# THE BILLIONAIRE'S FAKE FIANCEE

J. S. COOPER

# The Billionaire's Fake Fiancée

# ABOUT

I pretended to be the girlfriend of one of the richest men in New York City.

It was only meant to be the one time. It was the week before Christmas, I was shopping with my best friend, and we were hungry and wanted to dine at a swanky new restaurant on the Upper West Side.

But the hostess misunderstood me when I mentioned Max Parker's name. I'd been complaining that he was the reason why I'd lost my job. Who was I to correct her when it meant that "my relationship" had caused a table to suddenly open up?

And then the next week I accidentally let it slip that Max Parker was my boyfriend to get into an exclusive club. And then there was the time when I saw that Chanel handbag and Prada shoes. I mean, it didn't really hurt anyone, did it? It was just a little white lie.

How was I to know that my fake boyfriend would find out that I'd been using his name? Now he's blackmailing me into playing his fake fiancée in an arrangement that could only be classified as risqué. Turns out if I want to keep my apartment and not move home with my parents, I'm going to have to play along with his game. Only he's going to have to go along with my rules as well, and he doesn't know that I've got a plan of my own.

This book is a work of fiction. Any resemblance to actual persons, living or dead, or actual events is entirely coincidental. Names, characters, businesses, organizations, places, events, and incidents either are the product of the author's imagination or are used fictitiously.

Copyright © 2020 by J. S. Cooper

Thank you for purchasing a J. S. Cooper Book. You can join my mailing list here to receive a free book.

# PROLOGUE

"Excuse me, are you Charlotte Johnson?" A deep voice came from behind me.

Startled, I jumped as I walked into my apartment building.

"Yes?" I turned around cautiously, looking at the man behind me. He had a New York Yankees baseball cap on and dark sunglasses. I studied him for a few seconds trying to recognize him, but he was covered up so well that I could barely make out his face. "Can I help you?"

"I'm with the *New York Post,* and I wanted to ask you some questions."

"Questions?" I blinked and swallowed hard. Oh shit! "Questions about what?"

"About your relationship with Max Parker," he said confidently and quietly. "Do you mind if I interview you?"

"Uhm, yes, I mind." I thought quickly. "Unfortunately, I'm not in a position to talk to the press at this time."

"Oh?" He cocked his head to the side. I wished that he would take his glasses off so I could see his eyes.

"Yes, he's a very private man, and our, uhm, relationship is so new that he, uh, doesn't want us to ruin it by talking to the press."

"So you're confirming that you are dating him?"

"Well, I don't like to say anything." I bit down on my lower lip. "How do you know I'm dating him?"

"Didn't you see the article today?" He held up a newspaper for me to see, and my heart stopped as I read the headline.

"What article?" I said stupidly as if I wasn't looking at the paper right in front of me.

"The article about you and Max Parker ..." He paused for a few seconds, clearly wondering if I was as thick as two bricks. "And the fact that you're on the way to an engagement."

"What?" My jaw dropped. This had really gotten out of control.

"I wanted to know if this was a shotgun wedding?"

"Shotgun?" My heart was racing now.

"Are you getting married because you're pregnant?"

"Pregnant?" I tried not to laugh. *No, I'm not pregnant—I've never even met the guy!* I wanted to shout at the man in front of me, but I didn't dare say anything.

"Is it true that he has a ten-inch cock?"

"Excuse me?" Had he just said *cock*? What sort of reporter asked these sorts of questions?

"I said is it true that he has a —"

"That is enough." I raised my voice and held my hand up. "You should watch how you're talking to me." The man lifted one eyebrow and smirked as I spoke. "My boyfriend, Max Parker, won't be happy to hear that you've been so rude to me."

"Your boyfriend or your fiancé?" The man took off his sunglasses and his eyes pierced into mine. "Why don't you call him now and see what he has to say?" His bright blue eyes seemed to be mocking me as he stared at me. As if he knew that there was no way for me to call Max Parker. And it was then that I recognized him from the club I'd been at the night before.

"You!" I pointed my finger at the man who had been so rude to me the night before. "It's you!"

"Yes." His lips curled up and his eyes mocked me. "It's me."

"Are you following me?" I tried to ignore the heat that had suddenly overtaken my body. I was not going to be attracted to this reporter, no matter how hot he was.

"Am I following you?" He cocked his head to the side. "I just want to get the story of the decade."

"Story of the decade?" I rolled my eyes. "I hardly think my love life is the story of the decade."

"No one cares about your love life." He shook his head and smirked again. "The real story here is how you trapped *the* Max Parker."

"That asshole deserves to be trapped," I muttered under my breath. "Preferably under a ten-ton elephant."

The man leaned forward. "Sorry, what? I didn't hear that."

"Nothing." I turned and hurried towards the elevator.

"Are you as kinky as he is?" He looked me over consideringly. "I heard he's into some really dirty stuff." He licked his lips slowly and deliberately, and I shivered slightly.

"I'm not talking to you anymore."

I could hear the man walking behind me, and my anger intensified. I prayed for the elevator to hurry up.

"Why don't you just leave me alone? I'm not interested in talking to the media!" I glared at him.

"Yes, I'm sure you're not." His voice was sarcastic. "I'll bid you adieu, Charlotte Johnson." He nodded his head and then grinned at me. "Until we meet again."

"I sure hope that that's never." I tilted my nose up and gave him my dirtiest look.

"Really?" He cocked his head to the side and grinned. "I've a feeling that we'll meet again." He looked me over and winked. "And you be sure to tell Max Parker that he owes you a spanking for being a naughty girl."

"Excuse me?"

Without warning, he leaned forward and kissed me on the lips, his mouth pressing possessively against mine. I couldn't stop myself from kissing him back and my body melted into his as his fingers played with my hair. When he pulled away from me, I was breathing hard.

He chuckled. "I said I think you better tell your boyfriend Max Parker you've been a very naughty girl." He winked again. "I don't think he would like to find out that you've been kissing strangers and giving them hard-ons."

He chuckled at my shocked expression and then walked away without another word. The elevator arrived with a loud *ding*, and yet I couldn't move.

I stood there, completely speechless.

# CHAPTER 1

Two Weeks Earlier

"Who the hell does Max Parker think he is?" I rolled my eyes at Anabel, my best friend, and continued moaning about the man who had ruined my life. "He thinks that he can just buy up businesses and fire people, just like that? He just doesn't care about humanity."

"Well, his job is to make money, not to care about people." Anabel offered me a small smile, her green eyes concerned as she reached over to grab my hand, carefully avoiding the large latte that sat in front of me on the small table. "But I agree with you, he's an asshole," she added quickly, knowing that I didn't need her to play devil's advocate. She knew how I felt about people who cared more about money than human lives. "How about we go and grab lunch and forget about him?" She took a sip of her green tea and gave me one of her sweet, placating smiles. Anabel was used to my mini-melt-downs, and while she always tried to be a voice of reason, she always had my back.

"I don't know." I sighed as I thought back to my bank

balance. I could picture the computer screen in my mind as I'd stared at the lonely sum of $206 in my checking account and $500 in my savings account. How the hell I had so little money after having worked full-time for two years was beyond me. I ignored the feeling of doom in my stomach as I wondered how I was going to pay my rent the next month.

Damn that Max Parker!

"Now that I don't have a job, I have to watch my spending," I said, ignoring the fact that I had three plastic bags full of clothes and soaps in my hands. Bath and Body Works had had a sale on today where I got six products for the price of five, so I could hardly say no. And clothes from Target and Old Navy didn't count as actual shopping. The total I'd spent was less than a designer suit. Plus, I'd used my American Express and could worry about the bill next month. It was almost like free money, plus if I included the points I was going to get, it was almost like I was getting paid for shopping. Almost.

"My treat," Anabel said with a wide smile as she grabbed my hand. "I owe you a birthday lunch, so let's just grab it today." Her bright green eyes looked into mine with such an encouraging, hopeful look that all I could do was smile back at her. Her long light brown hair hung down her back, and I tried not to envy her natural beauty. Anabel looked like a model. She was absolutely stunning and everywhere we went men stared at her, hoping for a chance—not that she ever gave them one. She was so completely focused on her career as a lawyer that love wasn't on her mind at all. She also seemed to be oblivious to the fact that she was so beautiful. It was crazy.

I, on the other hand, tried very hard each day to make sure I looked as good as I could.

"Hmm, okay," I agreed, even though she didn't owe me anything. For my birthday, she'd taken me to dinner and given

## THE BILLIONAIRE'S FAKE FIANCEE

me a bottle of Gucci perfume, but I wasn't going to argue with her. Anabel was making big bucks at a law firm, and if she wanted to take me out, who was I to say no? "If you're sure."

"Of course, I'm sure." She grinned. "I know just the place. It's this new restaurant that just opened up on 78th Street. There might be a wait, but we can look at photos of Max Parker online and stare at his balding hair and fat face and have a laugh. But I'm open to your suggestions as well."

"Hahaha, I bet he looks like a short, fat troll." I had no idea what Max Parker looked like, but I assumed all billionaires looked the same.

"I bet he does." Anabel grinned at me. "Oh, I should invite Emily. She's back in town."

"Yay! I was going to ask you if she was back."

Emily was Anabel's roommate and one of our mutual best friends from college. She was straight up and very honest and one of the funniest people I knew. If anyone could make me feel better about my day, it was Emily. Lunch with Emily and Anabel would be fantastic. They would get me out of my funk in no time. In college, we'd been known as "The BFF Gang" because where one of us went, the other two weren't far behind. I had been so caught up with what was going on with my job that I hadn't texted her to see if she was back yet, and that made me feel slightly guilty.

"Yup, she got back last night from her camping trip. Do you want to text her or should I?"

"You text her and I'll look up places. Let's try somewhere really swanky and fun. And then when she gets there we can go stare at pictures of that ugly loser, *Max Parker,* and curse him to hell."

I growled as I said his name. I would have punched him if I could. It all seemed so dreadfully unfair to me. This man had essentially lied to my bosses when he'd bought their small boutique design shop. He had said he would keep on all of the old staff and just expand the business. At least, that's what my boss of two years, Sally, had said when she'd sold off the company to the Parker Corporation. But he hadn't even waited a week before he'd fired all five employees, effective immediately. Right before we were meant to get our annual bonus and in the holiday season as well. Did he not know that Christmas was meant to be a holy season, a time to be a good person? Not that he cared.

I'd never met the man but I hated him. Hated him about as much as I'd ever hated anyone. I knew it was irrational, but I'd had plans for that Christmas bonus. Plans that meant something, and he'd gone and ruined them.

"Okay, Emily is in. She wants to know if you have a place in mind yet?"

I shook my head. "Still looking, sorry." I offered Anabel an apologetic smile. "I was killing Max Parker in my mind again."

"Soon, you'll have us hunting him down." She grinned at me and wiggled her eyebrows. "What we do after that, I don't know."

"Hmm, let's think."

"Well, Emily must be a pro with a gun after her camping trip." Anabel giggled. "I think she said she was going to hunt for her food."

"Emily? Hunting?" I burst out laughing. "Yeah, right. I thought she was going glamping?"

"I think she thought she was as well." Anabel's eyes widened in glee. "Turns out she was wrong. Wait until you hear about her trip. Let's just say, your day isn't so bad. You didn't almost shit on a rattlesnake."

"What? Oh, poor Emily!" I laughed and Anabel and I giggled together, picturing our flighty friend squatting down to use the toilet. "Oh, Anabel, you always know how to make me feel better." I shook my head and giggled again. "Hunt him down, indeed." I looked around surreptitiously to make sure no one had heard us, just in case we had some nosy neighbors. I could see two older ladies, with uptight expressions, looking at us from the corner of the coffee shop. We had been laughing loudly, and I'm sure they disapproved, but I didn't care. "He'd be so lucky."

"Yes, he would." A light appeared in her eyes. "He wishes he could have three hotties all over him."

"Yeah." I nodded. "Poor old man probably can't even get it up." I grinned. "You know what, let's try that swanky place you heard about. I'm having trouble concentrating on finding a place on Yelp. This will work out better."

"Awesome." Annabel texted quickly then looked at her watch. "Emily says she will meet us there in an hour. I have to get my legal secretary to send a file request to opposing counsel for a deposition hearing next week. Do you mind if I take my laptop out and do some work for the next ten minutes?" She gave me an apologetic look.

I shook my head. "Of course not." I smiled. "The fact that you dropped everything to come and have a coffee with me means everything. You really are my best friend, Ana."

I picked up my latte and took a sip before grabbing my notebook and a pen. I didn't want to get sappy, but I knew that Anabel understood why I was so upset. I flicked to the first page of the notebook and stared at a Polaroid photo of a grinning fifteen-year-old me sitting on Brandon's lap. He was laughing as well, his head back, and his eyes wide and there was glitter falling all around us. He'd thrown it as a practical joke. It had taken me weeks to get the glitter out of my hair, but I hadn't been mad. I was never mad with Brandon. Nothing he had ever done had ever upset me. Until the end. Then he'd just up and broken my heart. I quickly turned the page to stop looking at the photograph, as I didn't want to think about him now. I didn't want to get upset. I needed to focus on my future.

I was going to make a list of all the different types of jobs I was going to look for now I was out of work. I had been a junior graphic designer when I worked for Sally, but my true love was acting. Was now the time to try and make it as an actress?

I nibbled on my lower lip and tried to quash those thoughts. My parents would kill me if I told them that I was going to focus on that instead. They were helping me pay my student loans back, and I knew that they'd make me come back home if I didn't get a stable job. Even though, at twenty-five, I was far too old to have to do what they said. What twenty-five-year-olds went back home to live with their parents? I ignored the voice inside my head that was screaming. *Fools like you who try to become actresses with no savings—that's who, Charlotte*! I'd come to some sort of compromise. Maybe I could audition and find a part-time job, but it would have to be a job that paid me well enough to cover my rent and bills.

All of a sudden, I didn't feel so good about my new $2000 a month apartment overlooking Central Park. At the time, it had seemed like a steal. It was almost unheard of to have your own apartment overlooking the park. Granted, it was only a studio, but I didn't care. A studio with no roommates was better than an apartment with roommates in my opinion. But now I had to figure out a way to get a job within 30 days that paid me well. I had very little work experience and a degree in history from Columbia. I sighed as I realized my options weren't looking too great at all.

CHAPTER 2

"**D**ominic's is popping, wow!" Anabel and I had arrived outside the exclusive new restaurant. There was a line of people waiting outside and three limousines parked outside. "Do you think we will get a table?" I asked her as we walked up to the door.

"I think so," Anabel said, but she looked unsure. "Oh look, there's Emily. Emily, over here!" She raised her voice and waved to Emily, who was leaning against the wall next to the restaurant. Emily grinned as she looked up and saw us and came running over, her long black hair bouncing against her back.

"There you are, girls." Emily gave us both a big hug as she reached us and her blue eyes stared into mine in concern as she pulled back. "You okay, Char?" She studied my face for a few seconds. "I heard you lost your job."

"Meh," I made a face. "I'm fine." I ran a hand through my long black hair and stifled a sigh. "Nothing a couple of stiff drinks won't fix," I said, and we all laughed.

"I'm going to go and see if I can get us a table." Anabel headed towards the door. "Wish me luck."

"You got this!" Emily's voice was enthusiastic. "If anyone can get us a table, it will be you, hot-shot lawyer."

As soon as her back was turned, Emily grabbed my hands.

"Okay, tell me everything. What the fuck happened? Didn't they just give you a promotion?"

"Yes," I said. "That's why I got my own place, remember?"

"Yeah, I remember. That's so shitty. So they just decided to fire you?"

"No, well, yes." I sighed and took a long breath. "I guess the company wasn't doing well, and Sally wanted to retire and move to Boca Raton in Florida. Some billionaire made an offer on the business and he promised to keep on all the staff, so she ended up selling it to him." I flushed, feeling angry as I told the story. "And then as soon as he took over, Parker Industries or Parker Corporation, whatever it's called, had their HR department send us all a letter firing us."

"Oh, no!" Emily's jaw dropped. "But can he do that? Can't you guys sue him?"

"Sue him?"

"Sue him for breaking his promise to Sally. Didn't he promise Sally?"

"It was verbally. It wasn't in their contract when she sold." I shook my head. "So I'm screwed, along with the others."

"Getting a severance package?" Emily looked at me hopefully.

"One thousand dollars." The words dripped off of my tongue like poison. "What the hell am I supposed to do with a grand?"

"Not much in New York City," Emily commiserated with me. "That's absolutely ridiculous. Want us to go and egg his car or send a stripogram to his office or something?"

"No." I laughed. "Though that would be funny."

"That would be hilarious. I'd totally do it with you. Most

probably Anabel wouldn't because she doesn't want to lose her law degree or whatever."

"I think she'd lose her bar license, not her degree, but yeah." I grinned at her. "I don't think we should risk getting arrested."

"You don't think we could talk our way out of a ticket?" Emily winked at me, and I just shook my head.

"What would you do to get out of a ticket, Emily?" I asked her knowing she would say something that would make me laugh.

"I wouldn't blow a cop, if that's what you're asking. That rumor was false." She gave me a wicked smile.

"What rumor?? You did not blow a cop to get out of a ticket?" I stared at her, my mouth agape.

"Of course I didn't, but wouldn't that be a totally awesome story if it were true."

"Oh, Emily." I laughed and looked towards the front of the restaurant to see Anabel walking back to us with a disappointed look on her face. "Oh no, looks like Anabel wasn't lucky."

"Oh no, we don't have a reservation?" Emily wrinkled her nose. "I looked up the menu and the food looks divine. Expensive but divine."

"We can't afford expensive." I grinned at Emily, who, even though she had a job, was almost as broke as me. "So maybe this was a sign for us to go to Shake Shack or something."

"Shake Shack. Hmmph." Emily rolled her eyes. "What's the word?" She asked Anabel, who joined us with a little shrug.

"They said we can wait to get a table, but there is no guarantee that one will become free."

"So we could be standing here for hours and still get no food?" I looked at Anabel and she nodded. "Well, that doesn't sound great."

"I have an idea." Emily's expression was devious. "Let's go inside by the hostess table and just stand there and talk very loudly about how hungry we are."

"I don't know." Anabel shook her head. "That seems a bit rude."

"Exactly! That's the whole point. They should seat us faster then because they won't want us making a scene." Emily linked both of our arms. "Come on, girls, it's the Christmas season, let's have some fun."

"Emily." Anabel tutted and gave me a look. I just grinned back at her and we all walked towards the restaurant, prepared to guilt them into giving us a table.

❧

THE SKINNY BLONDE HOSTESS SHOT US ANOTHER LOOK OF disdain as we assembled right next to her desk. I peeked into the restaurant and stared at some of the dishes on the table closest to us. One lady was eating some sort of lobster dish and her companion had a juicy steak that looked delicious. The smells emanating from the kitchen were mouth-watering, and my stomach was starting to grumble.

"So what are you going to do now?" Emily asked me as we stood there.

"Eat?"

"No, career-wise?"

"Oh, I don't know." I sighed. "I was hoping that Max Parker would grow a heart and come to his senses, but I don't think he cares."

"Yeah, billionaires think about money and not people." Emily nodded. "I think I've heard of him. Wasn't he married to Marilyn Monroe or something?"

"Who? Max Parker?"

"Yeah." She nodded. "I think so. He's the CEO of Parker Enterprises right? Don't they own half of Manhattan?"

"I suppose." I shrugged. "Old asshole."

"I bet he has a small dick," Emily said.

"Yup, shriveled up and small just like him." I giggled.

"With veins all over his legs," Anabel added. "What does he look like, anyways?"

"Hold on, let me check." I pulled out my phone and did a Google search. I went to images and surveyed the results. There weren't many and I clicked on what appeared to be an older photo. "Okay, well look at this," I said as I pulled up the article and clicked on the photo. "Oh, hot damn, look at that body!" I said as I showed Emily and Anabel the only photo of Max Parker I could find.

It was a photo of him on the Harvard website and was of him in his swimming trunks as part of the swim team. Apparently, Max Parker had been some sort of hotshot swimmer back in the day.

"He was a looker when he was young," I said in surprise, staring at his handsome face. I could tell from the grin on his face that he'd been a cocky asshole even then. He had that sort of self-assured smug grin that handsome men who came from money always had. Pompous asshole. "I wonder what he looks like now?"

"Girl, that photo is from ten years ago." Emily gawked at the screen. "He's not sixty-something. He has to be in his late twenties or early thirties now."

"You're right. I didn't even think about that." I looked at her in surprise. "You can tell he's one of those preppy assholes that we hate."

"Yeah, some trust-fund kid that thinks he owns the world." Emily nodded.

"Yup," I said, and we all looked at each other knowingly. We'd met many offspring of rich and famous people at

Columbia. While all three of us were Ivy-League-educated as well, we'd all come from modest upbringings, with our tuition being offset by scholarships and grants. "'I'm Max Parker, I'm the man, and I can have any woman that I want.'"

"Bet he has to pay for sex," Emily said.

I giggled while Anabel just shook her head at the two of us. I knew she disapproved of our making fun of him, and if I was honest, my heart wasn't really in it. But I hated entitled assholes who thought that money made the world go around. He hadn't even stopped to think about his new employees and how they were going to survive. He hadn't cared at all. We were just numbers to him. Numbers that didn't matter.

"Yup, if I met him he would be begging me for it," I said with a smirk. "Oh, Charlotte, please, please kiss me. Please let me go down on you. Please let me pleasure you." I paused. "And then I would say, Max Parker, I wouldn't let you near me if you gave me ten billion dollars." My voice rose. "You can beg me as much as you want, Max Parker, but I—"

"Excuse me," The blonde hostess approached us. "Did you just mention Max Parker?" She had a tight smile on her face.

"Sorry, what?" Heat crept into my cheeks. Had she heard what I said?

"I didn't mean to listen to your conversation, but I heard you saying that Max Parker had said something to you?" She looked at my face and then down at my clothes and I could tell from the look in her eyes that she doubted he'd ever had anything to do with me. Smug bitch! Just because I was wearing jeans from Old Navy didn't mean I couldn't date a billionaire.

"Well, my boyfriend, Max Parker, says many somethings to me." I looked at her haughtily. "In fact, I just got off the phone with him. I was telling him, that I was waiting in line at—"

"Oh, but I just wanted to let you know that a table was just made available." She looked at me with a panicked expression. "Your friend didn't say that you were acquaintances of Mr. Parker's."

"I wouldn't say we were acquaintances. He's my boyfriend."

"He's her man." Emily grinned gleefully. "And between us four, I think he's about to propose soon. He was sending me photos from Tiffany's asking me which one I thought Charlotte would like best."

"And I told you five carats was just way too big and ostentatious. I prefer a four-carat ring."

"You're to be engaged to Max Parker?" The blonde's eyes widened. "Why didn't you say so?"

"Everyone knows who I am already." I looked her over. "Well, everyone who's important."

"I'm so sorry. Please follow me." The blonde looked mortified as she motioned us to follow her.

"What's going on?" Anabel mouthed to me.

I just shrugged. "Come on."

I grinned at Emily and followed behind the blonde bitch, strutting my stuff as if I really and truly was the girlfriend of a billionaire. I didn't feel any shame in my little white lie.

The other two followed behind me and I could have bet what the expressions on their faces were without even seeing them. Emily was likely grinning; she loved mischief. Anabel was probably trying hard to look dignified and not totally embarrassed. She was the most straight-laced of all of us, but she still went along with our shenanigans. I was the boldest and brazen of the group, most of the time. Maybe it was because I wanted to be an actress, but I swore that I could get away with almost anything.

"I hope this table is to your pleasing, ma'am." The waitress stopped next to a central table that already had a bottle of Champagne sitting on ice. "Please accept today's meal and drinks on the house."

"Hmm, I suppose I can do that."

"I do hope that you won't tell Mr. Parker that you had to wait." She offered me a small smile. "We didn't know ..." Her voice trailed off as I gave her a steely look.

"No, I suppose you didn't." I paused for a few seconds and looked at my two friends, whose faces were shocked. "I won't tell Maxy what's happened today. I wouldn't want to upset him, you know. And he would be *very* upset if he knew."

I walked towards my chair and the blonde girl pulled it out from the table for me and then pushed me in. Emily and Anabel sat down quickly and we were then presented with menus.

Two seconds after the blonde lady walked away we all burst into giggles with Anabel just shaking her head.

"Oh, Charlotte, how could you pretend to be his girlfriend?" she asked me with a small frown.

"It's not like I came here planning to lie, but then the opportunity presented itself." I gave her a winning smile. "Plus this is nothing. It doesn't even hurt him. He owes me a lot more than a free meal at a restaurant."

"A very nice swanky restaurant," Emily added.

"It's still just food." I shrugged. "He owes us more than that. Let's drink, eat and be merry. It's on me." I winked and we all giggled once again before we gave our full attention to the menus.

## CHAPTER 3

"Do you like my handbag?" I did a little spin as I showed off my handbag to Emily and Anabel the next day.

"Is that Chanel?" Anabel's jaw dropped as I grinned. "Charlotte, how can you afford a Chanel handbag? Did you get your job back?"

"No, I didn't get my job back." I made a face. "In fact, the office space is up for sale." I gave her a pointed look. "Turns out Max Parker had no intentions in even keeping the business open. He just wanted the property." I shook my head. "He's an even bigger asshole than I thought."

"So how did you get the bag?" Anabel pressed on, looking at me with a small frown.

"Oh, does it matter?" I shrugged and looked at Emily. "Isn't it beautiful?"

"It's gorgeous." She nodded and reached out to touch it. "I can't believe you have a Chanel. It looks vintage."

"It is vintage." I grinned. "I got it in the Village. And I only had to pay $100."

"How did you get it for $100?" Anabel looked suspicious.

I smiled, a little guiltily. "Okay, so I *might* have started talking about my boyfriend and how he was looking to invest in some boutiques."

"What boyfriend?" Anabel prodded, always the lawyer.

"You know." I made a face and licked my lips nervously.

"You didn't say Max Parker was your boyfriend again, did you?" She shook her head disapprovingly. "Charlotte, you cannot go around town telling people that Max Parker is your boyfriend. You don't even know him."

"Who cares?" I shrugged. "No one is ever going to find out."

"It's a lie, Charlotte." Anabel sighed. "Lies always catch up to people."

"Fine, I won't do it again." I pouted. "I mean, honestly it's not hurting anyone, and really, Max Parker owes me a lot more than a free lunch and a Chanel bag." I looked at Emily for support. "What do you think, Em?"

"I agree." She nodded. "What can it hurt?" She smiled at me. "He'd be lucky to be dating you."

"Yeah, I mean, an asshole like him wishes he could be with someone like me."

"Uh huh." Anabel rolled her eyes and then took a seat on my small couch. "You're going to get yourself into trouble if you keep lying."

"I wasn't *lying* lying." I made a face. "But fine. So are we all going out tonight?" I looked at my two friends. "Let's see if we can meet three hotties and have some fun."

"I'm down," Emily said with a grin. "We deserve to have some fun."

Anabel looked reluctant. "I'm supposed to work tonight."

"Oh, Anabel. You're always working." I gave her pleading look. "Let's just go out tonight and have fun."

"Oh, Charlotte." She grinned at me and shook her head. "Fine, but you two are bad influences on me."

"What? Why me?" Emily laughed as she sipped from the glass of wine I'd given her. "I'm a good girl."

"Uh huh." Anabel sat down on the couch next to her and laughed. "You're an even bigger trouble maker than Charlotte."

"Hey." I stuck my tongue out at her and sat down on the oversized beanbag across from them. "I'll have you know that I'm very mature and responsible."

"So where are we going to go tonight?" Emily looked excited. "I can't tell you the last time I went out."

"That's because you're in a relationship with Netflix." I laughed.

"So are you!" Emily shot back at me.

"How is it that we are three hot girls that are all single?" I asked and took a huge sip of wine. "We need to find men."

"I don't need a man." Anabel made a face. "I have my job."

"I have pizza and my vibrator." Emily giggled. "Both make me feel very satisfied."

"Well, I need more than a vibrator." I played with my ponytail. "I want a man that can have me screaming his name all night long while he tugs on my hair."

"Have you been reading those romance books again?" Emily stared at me. "When have you ever had sex with a man that had you screaming his name even once?"

"I've screamed before." I laughed. "Well, maybe not screamed, but gotten loud."

"I can't remember the last time I've screamed." Emily sipped on her wine again. "To be honest, a man has never made me scream. Shit, I don't even know if I've had a real orgasm yet."

"That's because you haven't had sex with a real man." Anabel's voice was almost dreamily. "Trust me, when you have an orgasm, you'll know it."

"She's talking about her long lost love again." Emily rolled her eyes and gave me a look. "He who shall not be named."

"More like he who has never been named," I said. Anabel blushed. "Are you ever going to tell us about this mysterious lover of yours?"

"No." She shook her head. "He's not important."

"Well, he must be somewhat important if memories of sex with him are your best sexual memories."

"That's all it was." She shrugged and jumped up. "So what are you guys going to wear tonight?"

Emily and I both made a face at each other. We'd all been best friends since our freshmen year at Columbia, yet Anabel had never once told us about the man who had been her first lover and first love.

"Let's get all dressed up and have some fun. We can get drunk and flirt and who knows maybe one of us will get lucky." I bounced around in the beanbag. "Tonight we can have some fun, and then tomorrow I'll start looking for a new job."

"Ooh, we can go to this swanky new club in the Village." Emily looked excited. "I heard it's full of actors and stuff." She looked at me. "Maybe you can meet someone who will give you an audition?"

"I'll audition, all right." I giggled and danced around waving my hands back and forth in the air. "Romeo, Romeo, wherefore art thy bed?"

"Ha ha," Emily started laughing. "Juliet, I compare thee to a summer's day, now get on your knees and service me."

"You two are so ridiculous. You know that right?" Anabel laughed as well. "This is why we're single."

"Because we're fabulous?" I jumped up. "Let me show you the dress I was thinking of wearing tonight." I walked over to my closet and searched for the red dress I'd gotten a couple

THE BILLIONAIRE'S FAKE FIANCEE

of years previously but had never gotten to wear. I pulled it out of the closet and held it up.

"Where's the dress?" Emily grinned at me. "That looks sexy as hell."

"It's totally slutty." I grinned back. "Slutty enough for sex in a club with some tall, dark stranger."

"Yeah, right." Anabel rolled her eyes. "Charlotte, you're all talk. You wouldn't even bump and grind with a stranger, let alone have sex."

"You never know." I laughed, though she was correct. I was way too shy to actually do anything that crazy, but I loved to talk about some sort of exciting dalliance. Emily was just the same. The way she went on you'd think she was a sex addict, but she spent more time in front of the TV than she did going out on dates. "If I wear this, you both have to dress up as well."

"Okay." Anabel smiled. "I'm in, but Em and I should go home now so we can start getting ready."

"Meet us downtown at 8?" Emily smiled at me. "I'll text you the address."

"Sounds good. I can't wait."

They both downed the rest of their wine and made their way to the door. I gave them a little wave, and when the door closed I sank onto the couch and grabbed my handbag again. It really was beautiful, all shiny soft black quilted lambskin leather with chunky gold straps. I stared at the signature Chanel C's and smiled as I held the handbag to me. I couldn't believe I'd gotten it for $100. It had been a steal. And even though I shouldn't even have spent $100, how could I walk away?

I closed my eyes and tried to ignore the slight racing of my heart that told me that I was a shopaholic and a liar. I could still picture the owner's face in the boutique, as I'd gone on and on about my boyfriend, Max Parker, who'd asked me to find some good boutiques to invest in. I'd totally played it up, a lot more than I'd admitted to Anabel. I mean, was it my fault that I was such a good actress? Though I knew my success had more to do with me dropping Max's name than with my acting skills.

I put the handbag back down on the couch and grabbed my phone to see if I had any new texts or emails from Sally about a new job. She felt bad for the five of us who had been let go so suddenly and had said she'd see if she could find us new jobs, but I knew that was unlikely. How many graphics teams needed a graphic designer with very few design skills? I couldn't even really find my way around Adobe without watching YouTube videos, though Sally hadn't minded. I'd been hired because she'd liked the way I got really animated during presentations and she felt like my energy was positive and helped us land jobs, but I knew no recruiter was going to be impressed by that fact. Why hadn't I tried to learn a few more skills? My options with a history degree were very limited. I could try and become a teacher, but that would mean taking qualification tests, or I could try and work retail, though I didn't know what retail job was going to pay me enough to cover my rent and bills.

I groaned and felt like crying. I was up a creek without a paddle and the next step would have to be calling my parents. And I knew what they would say: "Get your ass out of NYC and come back home." Though my mom would never let my dad say "ass."

I couldn't let that happen. I didn't want to leave my friends or my apartment or New York. If only I really had a rich boyfriend. Then he could pay for my apartment. I had contemplated becoming an escort for a couple of months. I was young, pretty enough, and Ivy League-educated; surely I'd be a hit—but then I thought about having to go on dates with gross old men, and I shuddered. I wasn't whoring myself out to some old grandpas for a few bucks. Because let's be real, no self-respecting hottie would be using an escort service. It was only in books and movies that the sexy hot man was somehow using the escort service by mistake or whatever. In real life, it was old, balding men with drooping balls that wanted to pay girls like me. No thanks. I'd rather be back home, looking through the Coupon Saver magazine each week for deals on groceries before we headed to Publix.

I shuddered at the thought of going back to that life. To memories of Brandon. I couldn't do that to myself. I needed to get my act together.

# CHAPTER 4

"I'm too sexy for this dress, too sexy for this dress, I don't care that I'm a mess," I sang as I walked down the street with a little pep in my step.

I was determined to have a good night and just let my hair down. I was already trying to be a good girl and had taken two subway trains to get to the club address that Emily had sent me, even though a cab would have been much faster. I had decided that I would look for personal assistant jobs the next day and take an acting class in the evening. I was also going to stop using Max Parker's name to get perks. I had been a little dishonest with Anabel in that I'd used his name a couple more times than she knew about, but not for anything major. I mean, a large discount on a handbag, an even larger discount on some Jimmy Choo heels (that I was wearing tonight), and a discounted subscription to the *New York Times* (hey, I needed to find a job)—that wasn't that bad. I was almost positive that some women would have used their relationship to get free cars and free jewelry. But had I done that? Nope! Not even close.

# THE BILLIONAIRE'S FAKE FIANCEE

"Hey, sexy!" Emily whistled at me as I approached the club.

I ran to her and Anabel and gave them both a huge hug. "Why, hello, girls!" I looked them over. Emily was wearing a tight black dress that left nothing to the imagination and Anabel was in a silver glittery dress that had long slits up the legs. "We are hot."

"We sure are." Emily grinned and did a little shimmy. "Are we ready to dance?"

"I'm ready like Freddy." Anabel nodded and played with her long hair. It looked blonder than it had the other day and I wondered if she'd gotten highlights.

"Come on, girls." I sashayed towards the front of the club and smiled at the two stocky bouncers by the door. Both men looked tough and serious, like they could be ex-military. "Hi, guys, do you need to see our ID's?"

"You on the list?" The guy on the right said in what sounded like a Russian accent.

"The list?" I said, smiling widely and trying to flirt. "Do we need to be on a list?"

"Tonight is an exclusive party. You have to be on the list."

"Oh." I pouted and looked at Emily and Anabel. Emily was playing with her hair and flirting with the other bouncer, an African-American guy who didn't seem to care that he was in the presence of three hot young things. "I *think* we might be on the list." I pushed my breasts out towards the Russian bouncer. "Da," I said, hoping to impress him with what I thought was a Russian word.

He didn't blink. "Name?"

"*My* name?" I said and pursed my lips.

"Yes, your name."

"Can you help us?" I turned to the other guy who was standing there like a rock. He just stared back at me unspeaking, and I could feel my good mood leaving me. Were we not even going to get into the club?

"Give me your name and I'll check the list." The guy in front of me folded his arms and I pursed my lips.

"Well, my boyfriend Max Parker said he would make sure I was added to the list." I could hear Anabel groaning behind me. One last time! What could it hurt?

"Name?" The Russian guy asked, not seeming to recognize Max Parker's name.

"Charlotte Johnson," I said with all the attitude I could muster. "I'm a guest of Max Parker." I raised my voice this time and noticed that the other security guy was suddenly paying me more attention.

"You're Max Parker's girlfriend?" he grunted, and I nodded. I pulled out my phone and frowned.

"What are your names? I need to text Max to get this sorted."

"No need, ma'am." He smiled at me then. "Any guest of Max's is welcome." He looked me over and then he looked at Emily and Anabel. "Let them in, Vlad." He nodded. "Have a good night, ladies. Welcome to Fine & Rarest."

"Thank you!" I linked arms with Emily and Anabel. "Come on, girls, let's have some fun." I beamed at them both. Emily was grinning back but Anabel looked slightly upset. "First drink is on me," I promised as we made our way into the main room.

The room was already packed with Wall Street–looking types and lithe models. There was a DJ in the corner of the room spinning records and music pulsed throughout the room. Two scantily clad girls danced in cages next to the DJ booth, and there cocktail waitresses made their way through the crowd with glasses of colorful shots. "This is so cool," I said. I was about to make my way to the bar when someone tapped me on the back.

# THE BILLIONAIRE'S FAKE FIANCEE

"Hello, there." A tall man with a narrow face peered at me. "Did I just hear that you were dating Max Parker?"

"Sorry, what?" I stood still not knowing what to say.

"I was in the line behind you. You told those security guards that you were Max Parker's girlfriend. Can I ask if he'll be here tonight?" The man looked excited now.

"Oh, I don't know. This isn't really his kind of thing." I shook my head. "Sorry."

"Oh, okay." He looked disappointed. "I was really want to have a talk with him about an IPO that I ..." His voice trailed off and he shrugged. "Well, you don't want to know all the details. I've been trying to get a meeting with him, but his secretary keeps telling me that he's booked up."

"He's a very busy man." I nodded. "Very busy."

"Hmmm." He looked at me again. "You're not his normal type, are you?"

"What does that mean?" I said, glowering at him.

"I mean you're pretty, but ..." His voice trailed off. "Not exactly a Giselle, are you?"

"Now I know why Max doesn't call you back. You're not worth his time." I glared at him, wishing I had a drink in my hand so I could throw it in his face.

"You okay?" Anabel asked me as we walked away. "I'm mad at you, but I'm not going to shout at you after that prick said what he did."

"I'm fine." I shrugged. "He's a loser. What the hell did he mean by I'm no Giselle?"

"No idea, but he wasn't exactly a Leonardo DiCaprio." Emily looked back at the guy. "Shit, he's not even an Adrien Brody."

"Yeah, he sucked." I stopped by the bar and waved the bartender over to me. "Three Manhattans, please," I said as he stopped in front of me. "And make them strong, please."

"Anything for you, doll," he responded with a little wink,

and I grinned at him. He looked like he was about twenty-one, but he was absolutely gorgeous. Much better than the skinny-ass prick I'd just spoken to.

"Thanks."

Emily was dancing to the music and looking around the club. I looked around and saw a small group of men chatting. There were definitely a lot of movers and shakers at the club tonight. I was pretty sure I recognized one of the men from TV.

"Hey." I nudged Anabel. "Is that the mayor?"

"The mayor?" Anabel looked across the room and her jaw dropped. "Yes, and not only is that the mayor, but he's standing with the governor and Jackson Mondrian."

"Who?"

"The speaker of the house." She looked at me with wide eyes. "Charlotte, I don't think we should be here. I don't think this is the sort of exclusive event we want to be at."

"Oh my God, I just saw William Fences, the owner of that software company." Emily looked at us excitedly. "We're totally hobnobbing with the rich and famous!"

"Ooh." I bit down on my lower lip and grabbed the drinks the bartender had just handed me. "Take these, girls." I handed them their glasses and gave the bartender my credit card. "Look, let's drink and dance, and if it's not our scene we can leave, deal?"

"Fine." Anabel took a swig of her drink. "Let's go closer to the DJ booth and just have some fun. We deserve it."

"Yes, we do." I quickly signed the receipt, took a large gulp of my cocktail, and then started moving my body in time to the Lizzo song that had started playing, "That Bitch."

I shouted along with the song as I moved past my friends and I could see a couple of the Wall Street guys checking us out admiringly. This, of course, caused me to start swinging my hips just a little bit more and I added a couple of twirls as

THE BILLIONAIRE'S FAKE FIANCEE

I made my way over to the DJ. The skinny models were staring at me with disdainful looks, but I didn't care. They may have been magazine beautiful but they didn't look like they were having fun.

"Come on, Emily!" I grabbed her hand and spun her in a circle. "I love you!" I said as she spun and then went down to the ground, shaking her long dark hair around. She grinned at me and kept dancing.

"Love you, too," she said. "I got boy problems." She winked at me as she sang, and I couldn't stop myself from laughing.

"You and me, honey."

"And me, too." Anabel started dancing with us as well. She closed her eyes and started swaying back and forth, and a spark of happiness ignited in me. I was here with my friends, and I was having fun. There was nothing more important in my life than living my life and having special moments with my best friends. This was why I never wanted to go back home. Emily and Anabel were not my blood, but they were my family.

We stood there dancing and we all started screaming and jumping up and down when Ed Sheeran's "Shape of You" started playing. I threw my head back and sang my heart out as I danced. I could see the skinny asshole staring at me from across the room and I resisted sticking a finger up at him. He was speaking to some guy, and I wasn't sure if he was pointing at me or not. The man next to him was looking at me with a curious expression on his face and I flipped my hair and turned around. He was probably another loser who wanted to try and use me because he thought Max Parker was my boyfriend.

I finished up my drink and then decided to get another drink. "You guys want another?" I asked Emily and Anabel as they danced around. I motioned to the bar and then headed to get another drink. The club was now more packed and there was a wait to get drinks. I patiently stood behind two guys and nodded my head in time to the music as I waited.

"Hi." A man was suddenly next to me and peering down into my face.

"Hi," I said as I looked up at him. He had the most amazing blue eyes I'd ever seen in my life and I was slightly taken aback.

"Waiting on a drink?"

"Looks like it." I turned my head away from him as I realized he was the same guy I'd seen with the skinny tall guy.

"Do you come here often?" He moved closer to me and I looked over at him again. He was tall, easily six feet tall, with a fit, muscular build. His dark hair was neatly trimmed and his blue eyes gazed down at me. "Or only on nights your boyfriend isn't here?"

"My boyfriend?"

"I heard you were dating Max Parker." He looked me over carefully. "Or is that not true?"

"Well, of course it's true. Why would you think it's not true?" My face grew hot.

"So you're dating *the* Max Parker of Parker Corporation?"

"Is there another Max Parker that you know of?" I rolled my eyes at him as I started playing with my hair. "Look, I can't get you a meeting with him if that's what you want."

"You think I want a meeting with him?" His lips curled up as he stared at me.

"Why else are you asking me these questions?"

"How long have you been dating him?"

"None of your business." I glared at him. "I don't even know you."

"I could say the same." He smirked.

"Could say the same about what?"

"I could say that I don't even know you, either."

## THE BILLIONAIRE'S FAKE FIANCEE

"Well, that's good for both of us. Neither one of us knows the other." I tried to ignore the fact that he was one of the best looking guys I'd ever seen in my life. He also smelled so good. I just wanted to lean forward and breathe him in, but I wasn't a total creeper.

"Your name is Charlotte?"

I froze as he said my name.

"How do you know?"

"Well, doesn't everyone know that Max Parker's girlfriend's name is Charlotte?"

*Not Max Parker,* I thought to myself. "Well, we're a private couple, so ..." My voice trailed off and I gave him a dirty look. "He wouldn't really like knowing I was here talking to you about him."

"He's protective of your relationship?"

"He's very protective of me, and I am of him as well. I don't like people trying to take advantage of him."

"I assume that's so you can be the only one?"

My jaw dropped at his sarcastic tone. "Excuse me, I don't know who you think you are, but I don't appreciate your comments. I am with Max because, well, we get on well and he's, uh, a good lover." My face was bright red now. What the hell was I saying?

"He's a good lover, eh?" He grinned at me. "Would you go on the record saying that?"

"On the record?" I blinked at him and immediately fell still as his fingers touched my hair for a few seconds. His eyes came closer to mine and for one brief second I thought he was going to kiss me, but he didn't. Instead, he just stared into my eyes for what seemed like an eternity.

"Have a nice evening, Charlotte," He took a step back. "I hope you and your friends have a good time."

"My friends?" I sounded like a robot.

"The two women you were dancing with. I assume they're

your friends or wait, don't tell me—they're Max Parker's girlfriends as well and you're all in one big polyamorous relationship?"

"What? No! Max and I are monogamous."

That was it. I was never telling the lie again. I didn't care anymore what perks I'd miss out on. This was getting too tricky. What if one of these people told Max Parker that I was going around telling people I was his girlfriend? And then what if he told them he never knew me? How awful would that be?

"Well, tell him I said hello." He gave me a nod and walked away from me.

I wanted to call back to him and say that I didn't know his name, and without his name, how could I tell Max he'd said anything? But of course I didn't because it didn't really matter, did it? Whether I knew his name or not made no difference, I wasn't going to be telling Max Parker anything anyways.

CHAPTER 5

I had three missed calls from both Emily and Anabel on my phone, but I didn't call or text them back. I was too tired from hitting up employment agencies all day. I hadn't realized that I'd have to take typing tests as well as Word and Excel proficiency tests just to register to be an assistant. The day had gone disastrously, and I had a bad feeling that none of the recruiters had been impressed with my skills. I hurried towards my apartment building feeling glum.

As soon as I got inside, I was going to run a bath and make myself a grilled cheese sandwich. That would make me feel better. Then I'd text the girls to see what they had to say. Hopefully, they'd had a better day at work than I had. We'd stayed out way too late and gotten way too drunk the previous evening, but it had been fun. I smiled as I thought back to the handsome Italian guy I'd spent most of the night dancing with. He'd even wanted to come home with me, but I hadn't let him. He was on a plane back to Milan in the next couple of days and as much as I wanted to get laid, I didn't want to have a one-night stand with a man I would never seen

35

again. I stifled a yawn as I made my way to the apartment building and hurried towards the door.

"Excuse me, are you Charlotte Johnson?"

The deep voice came from behind me and I jumped out of fright as I walked into my apartment building.

"Yes?" I turned around cautiously, looking at the man behind me. He had a New York Yankees baseball cap on and dark sunglasses. I stared at him for a few seconds trying to recognize him, but he was covered up so well that I could barely make out his face. "Can I help you?"

"I'm with the *New York Post,* and I wanted to ask you some questions."

"Questions?" I blinked and swallowed hard. Oh, shit! "Questions about what?"

"About your relationship with Max Parker," his voice quiet and confident. "Do you mind if I interview you?"

"Uhm, yes, I mind." I tried to think quickly. "Unfortunately, I'm not in a position to talk to the press at this time."

"Oh?" He cocked his head to the side. I wished that he would take his glasses off so I could see his eyes.

"Yes, he's a very private man and our uhm, relationship is so new that he, uh, doesn't want us to ruin it by talking to the press."

"So you're confirming that you are dating him?"

"Well, I don't like to say anything." I bit down on my lower lip. "How do you know I'm dating him?"

"Didn't you see the article today?" He held up a newspaper for me to see and my heart stopped as my eyes took in the bold black words on the cream page.

"What article?"

"The article about you and Max Parker ..." He paused for a few seconds. "And the fact that you're on the way to an engagement."

# THE BILLIONAIRE'S FAKE FIANCEE

"What?" My jaw dropped. This had really gotten out of control.

"I wanted to know if this was a shotgun wedding?"

"Shotgun?" My heart was racing now.

"Are you getting married because you're pregnant?"

"Pregnant?" I tried not to laugh. *No, I'm not pregnant, I've never even met the guy!* I wanted to shout at the man in front of me, but I didn't dare say anything.

"Is it true that he has a ten-inch cock?"

"Excuse me?" Had he just said *cock*? What sort of reporter asked these sorts of questions?

"I said is it true that he has a —"

"That is enough." I raised my voice and held my hand up. "You should watch how you're talking to me." The man lifted one eyebrow and smirked as I spoke. "My boyfriend, Max Parker, won't be happy to hear that you've been so rude to me."

"Your boyfriend or your fiancé?" The man took off his sunglasses and his eyes pierced into mine. "Why don't you call him now and see what he has to say?" His bright blue eyes seemed to be mocking me as he stared at me. As if he knew that there was no way for me to call Max Parker. And it was then that I recognized him from the club I'd been at the night before.

"You." I pointed my finger at the man that had been so rude to me the night before. "It's you."

"Yes." His lips curled up and his eyes mocked me. "It's me."

"Are you following me?" I tried to ignore the heat that had suddenly overtaken my body. I was not going to be attracted to this reporter, no matter how hot he was.

"Am I following you?" He cocked his head to the side. "I just want to get the story of the decade."

"Story of the decade?" I rolled my eyes. "I hardly think my love life is the story of the decade."

"No one cares about your love life." He shook his head and smirked. "The real story here is how you trapped *the* Max Parker."

"That asshole deserves to be trapped," I muttered under my breath. "Preferably under a ten-ton elephant."

"Sorry, what?" The man leaned forward. "I didn't hear that."

"Nothing," I muttered and hurried towards the elevator.

"Are you as kinky as he is?" He looked me over consideringly. "I heard he's into some really dirty stuff." He licked his lips slowly and deliberately, and I shivered slightly.

"Excuse me, I'm not talking to you anymore." I was getting angry as I prayed for the elevator to hurry up. "Why don't you just leave me alone? I'm not interested in talking to the media!"

"Yes, I'm sure you're not," he said, his voice sarcastic as he stood next to me. "I'll bid you adieu, Charlotte Johnson." He nodded his head and then grinned at me. "Until we meet again."

"I sure hope that that's never." I lifted my nose up in the air and gave him my dirtiest look.

"Really?" He cocked his head to the side and grinned. "I've a feeling that we'll meet again." He looked me over and winked. "And you be sure to tell Max Parker that he owes you a spanking for being a naughty girl."

"Excuse me?" I said, and then he leaned forward and kissed me on the lips, his mouth pressing into mine in a possessing way. I couldn't stop myself from kissing him back and I could feel my body melting into him as his fingers played with my hair. When he pulled away from me, I was breathing hard.

He chuckled. "I said I think you better tell your

boyfriend, Max Parker, you've been a very naughty girl." He winked again. "I don't think he would like to find out that you've been kissing strangers and giving them hard-ons."

He chuckled again at my shocked expression and then walked away without another word. The elevator arrived with a loud ding, and I couldn't move.

I stood there, completely speechless.

THE BATH WAS FORGOTTEN AS SOON AS I GOT INTO THE elevator. I immediately started a group chat with the girls and tried not to panic. I was in deep shit if journalists were showing up at my apartment and showing me newspaper articles. How the hell was there a newspaper article out about the relationship? Why me?

*Charlotte: Oh shit, guys. You will not believe what happened to me!!!!*
*Anabel: I bet I will.*
*Emily: What happened?*
*Anabel: Emily, don't pretend like you don't know.*
*Charlotte: You guys know?*
*Anabel: I told you that this would catch up with you.*
*Emily: We've been calling and texting you all day, hon.*
*Charlotte: I was looking for a job. How bad is it?*
*Anabel: What do you know?*
*Emily: It's not soo bad.*
*Charlotte: It IS so bad. A reporter. Well, I think he's a reporter. He was waiting for me by my apartment today. He had a newspaper and the newspaper had an article about me and Max dating ... UGH. Kill me now!*

*Anabel: I've seen five articles today stating you and Max are not only dating but also engaged.*

*Emily: Did you get engaged and not tell us? Sorry, not sorry. HAHAHA.*

*Charlotte: NOT FUNNY! Omg! What am I going to do?*

*Anabel: Immediately stop telling people you're dating Max. The only good thing is that there are no photos of you or Max Parker in any of the articles, so hopefully, it will just die down.*

*Emily: I kinda wanna know how the newspapers even know about you? And your existence.*

*Charlotte: I think it was this asshole reporter that I met at the club last night. He was asking me questions and then today he was asking me more questions.*

*Anabel: Please tell me that you didn't say anything to him.*

*Charlotte: ...*

*Emily: ... ????*

*Charlotte: Oh shit!*

*Anabel: Charlotte! What did you say?*

*Charlotte: I might have said something about our sex life being great or something.*

*Anabel: Oh lawd.*

*Emily: And here I thought you hadn't gotten laid in ages.*

*Charlotte: Emily! :P The reporter guy also asked me if I was pregnant or something.*

*Anabel: What did you say?*

*Emily: Oh shit, are you Mary #2? Is that blasphemous to say that?*

*Charlotte: I don't think I said anything. He kissed me before I could say anything really.*

*Anabel: WHAT?*

*Emily: WHOA! Shut the front door!!! The reporter kissed you?*

*Charlotte: Yes! It was weird. He's cute but creepy. It's all very strange.*

# THE BILLIONAIRE'S FAKE FIANCEE

*Anabel: Charlotte, this sounds like a hot mess. You just need to deny deny deny. Okay??*

*Charlotte: I'll just say that there was some confusion if asked again. I went on a few dates with a man named Max Parker, but it's not the same person?*

*Emily: That could work!*

*Anabel: No. Stop the lies. Your only comment from here on out is NO COMMENT. You hear me????*

*Charlotte: Yes.*

*Emily: The lawyer has spoken.*

*Anabel: This is serious, guys.*

*Charlotte: OH SHIT!!! OH SHIT!!*

*Anabel: What?*

*Charlotte:.....*

*Emily: What is it, Charlotte??*

*Charlotte:......*

*Anabel: Are you okay?*

*Charlotte: Max Parker just emailed me....I'm so dead.*

*Emily: OH MY GOD. You're dead.*

*Anabel: Worst case scenario. What did he say?*

*Charlotte: Hold on, let me copy and paste it. I need you guys to help me formulate a response. Or maybe I should just jump off the bridge. :(*

I put my phone next to me on the couch and sat back as I stared at the screen on my laptop. I wasn't sure why I'd decided to check my email while I was on the phone with the girls. Actually, that wasn't true. I was hoping that I'd have some sort of job offer. I didn't expect to see an email from Max Parker. I chewed on my lower lip and read the email again.

To: ArtyCharlotteJohnson@Gmail.com
From: MaxParkerCEO@Parkercorporation.com

Subject: We Need To Talk

*Dear Ms. Johnson,*

*It has come to my attention that you are spreading rumors about me. In fact, I would go so far as to say the lies you are spewing are libelous and could give me reason to sue. We are not in a relationship, no matter what you might be wishing. We are not engaged. We are not having a baby. And we have never had sex. No matter how badly you may wish it were so.*

*To remedy this situation, I require you to make a full retraction to the press and to pay me $10,000 in fines. The lady I am actually seeing was not too happy to see my name in the paper today.*

*Awaiting your response,*
*Max Parker (Not your boyfriend)*

I quickly opened the email on my phone and copied it into the group text and tried not to hyperventilate.

*Charlotte: Okay, how bad is this?*
*Emily: You're so screwed. WOW.*
*Charlotte: Thanks, Emily.*
*Anabel: I hate to be the bearer of bad news but Emily is right. He can ask you to give a retraction. Legally, you don't have to pay him anything right now, but if he were to sue you, he could get more in damages.*
*Charlotte: More? I don't have ten grand. I don't even have one grand.*
*Emily: Oh boy! What are you going to do?*
*Charlotte: Let me apologize and say it was all a mistake and see what he says.*
*Anabel: I suppose it can't hurt.*

To: MaxParkerCEO@Parkercorporation.com
From: ArtyCharlotteJohnson@Gmail.com

Re: We Need To Talk

*Dear Mr. Parker,*
*I am so sorry that you became involved in this unfortunate situation. I believe I was misheard. I didn't mean that I was dating you. Feel free to let your girlfriend see this email. And I hope all is well.*
*Charlotte Johnson*

To: ArtyCharlotteJohnson@Gmail.com
From: MaxParkerCEO@Parkercorporation.com
Re: We Need To Talk

*Dear Ms. Johnson,*
*I don't believe you were misheard. I have it on good authority that you clarified who you were supposedly dating many times. And you claimed the man was me. Please stop lying.*
*Or are you suffering from an illness that makes you incapable of telling the truth?*
*Max Parker*

To: MaxParkerCEO@Parkercorporation.com
From: ArtyCharlotteJohnson@Gmail.com
Re: We Need To Talk

*Dear Max Pecker,*
*Why would I lie about dating an insufferable, rude prick such as yourself? I can have any man I want. In fact, I was kissing a hottie just tonight.*
*Charlotte Johnson*

To: ArtyCharlotteJohnson@Gmail.com
From: MaxParkerCEO@Parkercorporation.com
Re: We Need To Talk

*Dear Charlatan Johnson,*

*You were kissing a hottie tonight and yet you're still in bed alone? Guess you couldn't seal the deal? Or maybe that kiss was also a figment of your imagination, just like our relationship?*

*Max Parker, CEO (Not your boyfriend)*

*To: MaxParkerCEO@Parkercorporation.com*
*From: ArtyCharlotteJohnson@Gmail.com*
*Re: We Need To Talk*

*Dear Small Pecker,*

*I'm in bed alone because I'm not a ho. It takes more than money and good looks to get into my pants. I guess you're alone because your money doesn't impress anyone.*

*Charlotte Johnson, Graphic Designer*

*To: ArtyCharlotteJohnson@Gmail.com*
*From: MaxParkerCEO@Parkercorporation.com*
*Re: We Need To Talk*

*Dear Loose Lips,*
*It impressed you.*
*Max Parker, CEO*

*To: MaxParkerCEO@Parkercorporation.com*
*From: ArtyCharlotteJohnson@Gmail.com*
*Re: We Need To Talk*

*Dear Can't Get it Up,*
*Stop emailing me. Don't worry. I won't tell anyone I'm dating you again.*
*Can't Touch This*

*To: ArtyCharlotteJohnson@Gmail.com*

*From: MaxParkerCEO@Parkercorporation.com*
*Re: We Need To Talk*

*Dear Don't Want to Touch That,*
*Maybe you should do some better research next time you decide to lie. Maybe then you'll know what your supposed boyfriend looks like. Or what a passionate kiss feels like.*
*Max Parker (The man you cannot have)*

*To: MaxParkerCEO@Parkercorporation.com*
*From: ArtyCharlotteJohnson@Gmail.com*
*Re: We Need To Talk*

*Dear Asshole,*
*GOODBYE*
*Charlotte Johnson*

I pressed send and closed my eyes. That had gone disastrously, but it really hadn't been my fault, had it? I looked back at the group chat and saw that Anabel and Emily had proceeded to give me better advice on what to email, but of course, I'd been impetuous and just gone ahead and emailed without thinking.

*Charlotte: Hey guys, can we talk tomorrow? I need to go to bed. I'm exhausted. :(*

I sent the text quickly and then turned my phone off and shut down my laptop. I didn't want to think about it anymore tonight. I wanted to take a hot bath, soak in some Epsom salts, and listen to John Legend.

I hurried to the bathroom and lit some candles as I ran the water. My thoughts drifted away from Max Parker and his emails and went to the mystery reporter who had kissed me.

What he had done had been a total violation, but I had loved it. Absolutely loved it. The feel of his lips against mine had been warm and firm, and I'd felt a thrill in my belly that I hadn't felt in a long time. It was a pity he was such an asshole. Otherwise, I might have enjoyed spending a night getting lost in his big, beautiful blue eyes.

CHAPTER 6

*Knock knock.*

The banging on my front door was getting louder and louder, and I groaned as I rolled off the couch and walked towards the front door. I'd been too tired to turn my couch into a bed the night before and had just snuggled into the couch cushions.

"I'm coming," I mumbled as I made my way over to the front door, wiping the sleep out of eyes. For a few seconds before I opened the door I froze as it struck me that I didn't know who was on the other side. What if it was Max Parker or a police officer coming to serve me with papers for a lawsuit or something? I opened the door with trepidation and let out a huge breath when I recognized the faces on the other side.

"There you are." Anabel looked annoyed. She and Emily stood at my front door, frazzled looks on their faces.

"What's going on? I was sleeping." I yawned then and motioned for them to come inside.

"We've been texting you all night and morning," Emily

said, looking more concerned than I'd ever seen her. "Your phone keeps going to voicemail."

"We were worried." Anabel closed the door behind her.

"I turned my phone off, and I've been sleeping. Why? What's happened now?" I groaned wondering if there had been more stories that had been published about Max Parker and me.

"Nothing that we know of," Anabel said. "We were just worried about you."

"We took off work to make sure you were okay," Emily said with a small smile. "I know you like to pretend everything is okay, but we all know how stressed out you get."

"Oh, guys." I blinked back tears. It was too early to be this emotional. "I'm okay. I'll find a job soon, and I'm sure this Max Parker thing will go away. It was my bad, but he kinda deserved it. He's really a huge asshole. I wouldn't have done this if he wasn't an asshole."

"What do opinions and assholes have in common?" Emily said suddenly.

"I dunno?" I shrugged.

"Everyone's got one." She started giggling and I smiled at her. "Okay, I might have messed the joke up a bit, but you know what I mean."

"Ha-ha, I know," I said, and then frowned at Anabel who was opening up my laptop. "What are you doing?"

"I'm checking your emails." She raised an eyebrow at me. "I want to know what you sent to Max."

"That's really invasive! You can't just check my emails without asking me."

"You wanna bet?" she said and then entered my password to get into my laptop. "The three of us have no secrets from each other."

"Well, that's not exactly true," I mumbled under my breath, but I didn't say anything else. Anabel had some sort of secret from us. She'd never told us the true story about her first love, and I knew that she wasn't telling us because it was something crazy as opposed to just hurting. She hadn't dated the guy since she was 18, and yet she still never said anything about him. I wanted to know more, but now was not the time to bring it up.

"Oh, Charlotte," she groaned as she looked up from my laptop. "How could you?"

"How could I what?"

"What did she do?" Emily asked eagerly. "Tell me! Tell me!"

"She sent Max Parker the most inappropriate emails possible." Anabel just shook her head and sighed. "How could you?"

"How could I? Did you read his emails? He was so bloody rude. He called me a charlatan!" My voice rose.

"But Charlotte ..." Anabel's voice drifted off. "Let's go and get coffee. I need a coffee."

"Did he send me another email?" I asked her, curiosity getting the better of me.

"No." Anabel shook her head. "And hopefully he doesn't send any more." She pursed her lips. "He's a powerful man, Charlotte. You can't just go around pissing off powerful men."

"What's he going to do? Get me fired?" I gave her a look and then rolled my eyes. "Oh, yeah, he already did that. Oops." Emily laughed but Anabel just shook her head at me. I gave them both a small shrug and sighed. "Look, I know I messed up. I was just so taken aback by his emails and I'm still upset that I have no job."

"You can't blame him for that for the rest of your life." Anabel looked at me with a stern expression. "Unfortunately, he doesn't owe you anything."

"I know he doesn't owe me anything," I shot back, defensively. "But you have to admit he did treat me horribly!"

"Yes, he did," Emily spoke up for me. "Now hurry up and get dressed. I'm starving. Breakfast is on me."

"You can't afford that, Em!" I looked at her through narrow eyes. Emily wasn't generally any better with money than I was.

"I have a Chase Freedom credit card, don't I?" She giggled. "Today I can afford anything."

"You guys are so irresponsible," Anabel tutted. "I will pay for breakfast, and if push comes to shove, I'll help you with your rent."

"But you have millions in student debt."

"I have two hundred thousand dollars in debt." She grimaced. "So, not quite millions."

"But you can't afford to pay my rent. You wouldn't be living with Emily if you could."

"Friends help friends." She gave me such a sweet and loving smile that I immediately felt ashamed of myself. "Now hurry up. I need coffee and some pancakes."

---

"Oh, I love Sarabeth's." I relaxed back into the seat and looked at the menu. "Should I get the lemon and ricotta pancakes or the crab cakes egg benedict?" I pondered aloud. I wanted both.

"Whatever you want." Anabel shrugged. "I'm going to get the braised short rib hash."

"Oh, that sounds yummy. Can I try it?" I asked her.

"Of course." She nodded.

"I have an idea," Emily said. "Let's get three separate dishes, and we can all try all of them."

"Yes!" I said. "That sounds great." I picked up my glass of water and took a quick sip before continuing. "I wanted to thank you both for taking today off. It means a lot to me. I know I've been a bit of a mess recently and ..." My voice trailed off as I looked around the restaurant. I had the distinct feeling that someone was watching me.

I turned all the way to the left then froze as I saw the reporter sitting at a table with two other men. All of them were wearing suits. Were they stalking me?

Before I could think about what I was doing, I jumped up and hurried across the restaurant to the man's table. I tried to avoid looking at his pink lips and his strong hands and instead looked at his face. Mistake. By the light of the day, he looked even more handsome than he had in the evening. I didn't know how it was possible, but his eyes looked even bluer than they had before. They were so dazzling and breathtaking that I found it hard to look away. But then he gave me his signature derogatory smile.

I glared at him. "You!" I said loudly, pointing at him. "Are you following me?"

"Excuse me?" He smirked. He didn't even have the decency to look guilty or embarrassed.

"Look, I know you want the story on me and my relationship." I didn't speak as loudly this time. "But you're not going to get it. I should report you to the newspaper reporters board of ethics."

"There's no such board," he said with a superior smile. "And I have no interest in your nonexistent relationship."

"My *nonexistent* relationship?" My voice rose and my jaw dropped. "Excuse me?"

"You're excused," he said and then turned back to his two companions. "Sorry about that. I think they must have let some nutters back into the wild recently."

"Nutters." I nudged him on the shoulder, surprised at how warm and hard it felt. "I am not a nutter!"

"What do you want, lady?" He turned again to look at me.

"You're following me. You were at my apartment last night, and now you're here. This is not a coincidence." I glared at him. "And I am not crazy, thank you very much."

"Taking bets?" He chuckled, and I glared at him even harder.

"You kissed me last night," I said. "Or did you forget that as well? Hmm, did you?"

"Oh, is that why you're here?" He stood up, his eyes sparkling. "Why didn't you say?"

"Say what?"

My heart skipped a beat as he leaned towards me. What was he doing? It didn't take me long to find out as his lips were pressing down on mine once again, and once again, I found myself melting into him.

Before I could blink he was pulling away from me.

"There you go my love, this should keep you warm for the next couple of years." He grinned at me. "Now go back and tell your friends all about it."

"How dare you?" I glared at him. "You cannot just go around kissing strangers!"

"You didn't say no."

"You didn't ask." I glared at him. "Rude."

"Did you not enjoy it?"

"I did not," I lied, my cheeks burning. "You owe me an apology."

"Do I?"

"Yes, you do." I stared at him for a few seconds and then added under my breath, "loser."

"What did you just say?" His eyes narrowed at me.

"Nothing."

"I don't believe that you're capable of saying nothing, Charlotte Johnson."

"How do you know my name? And how did you know where I lived?"

"It would be weird if I didn't know your name ..." He traced a finger across my lips.

"Why?" I said, resisting the urge to bite his finger.

"Because we're so intimate."

"We're not intimate. You're a stalker."

"You think I'm a stalker, charlatan?"

"What did you just say?"

"Nothing." He licked his lips.

"Look, I understand that as a reporter you feel the need to get the story, but there is no story here."

"I see." He pursed his lips. "Did you see the headline in the *New York Times* today?"

"What headline?" My breath caught and my heart started racing. "Not on the front page?"

"No, dear, not on the front page." He grabbed a newspaper from the table and pulled it open to what appeared to be the fifth page. He pointed to a section on the lower right.

Multi-billionaire Max Parker on the path to wedded bliss

"Oh, no," I mumbled, my mind racing. I was in big trouble.

"I take it congratulations are in order?"

"Well ..." I looked away from him. I had no idea what to say.

"Can I see the ring?"

"The ring?" I blinked. "Well, you know, it's being resized."

"Oh, really?"

"Yes," I snapped, and then my eyes narrowed. "Are you the one that wrote that article?"

"No, I source all of my articles first." He shook his head. "I didn't write anything."

I looked over my shoulder. Emily and Anabel were staring at me with dazed expressions, and I knew they were dying to know who this man was and why he was kissing me. "Well, let's just say I hope not to see you again, or I might have to press charges."

"You might have to press charges?" He looked amused. "Well, we can't have that then, can we?"

"No, we can't." I leaned towards him. "I'm going to let you off this one time, but if I see you again, I'm going to have to tell my fiancé, Max Parker." I gave him a look. "And you don't want to get on his bad side."

"No, I suppose I don't." He nodded. "Well, you tell him I said hello."

I turned away and was starting back to my friends when I heard him calling me.

"Oh, and Charlotte?"

"Yes?" I said as I looked back at him.

"You're going to want my name, aren't you? If you're going to tell your fiancé I said hello?"

"I suppose so." I tried to look disinterested. "What is it?"

"It's Max."

My heart stopped. "Max?" I said, my voice a whisper.

He stepped toward me. "Yes, it's me, Max. Max Parker. Your fake fiancé."

He whispered the last words into my ear, and I couldn't stop my knees from buckling and my body falling into him in shock. I'd really gone and made an idiot of myself, and I had no one else to blame.

CHAPTER 7

"Charlotte, Charlotte, are you okay?" Anabel was rubbing my shoulder as I opened my eyes slowly.

"Am I dreaming?" I mumbled as I looked at her concerned face, but immediately I knew I wasn't. Max Parker was standing there next to Emily staring at me with glittering eyes and a sardonic look on his face. "No, I guess I'm not."

"Are you okay?" Anabel held her hand to my forehead. "You fainted."

"I, uh, I ..."

I was speechless. I didn't know what to say. How could the blue-eyed man be Max Parker? All this time, he had known. He had known and he had made fun of me. And me, being the fool that I was, had gone right along with it.

"My car is out front. I can take you to the hospital," Max said authoritatively as he reached out to grab my arm. "Come, Charlotte."

"No, it's okay," I said, not budging. "I'll be okay."

"Who is your friend?" Emily asked with wide eyes and a grin on her face. "I'm Emily, I don't believe we've met."

"Hello, Emily, my name is Max. Max Parker. I believe you might have heard of me before."

"Ooh." Her eyes widened even more, and even Anabel looked shocked. "The Max Parker?" Emily mouthed at me, and I nodded.

"Thanks for everything, Max," I said quickly, scrambling to my feet. "My friends and I should get back to our table now."

I avoided his eyes. I could feel people staring at me from all around the restaurant now, but I just wanted to leave. I looked up and could see that his two male companions were looking at me with inquisitive eyes, and I wondered if they knew who I was.

"I think we need to talk, Charlotte." He pressed his lips together. "Just the two of us."

"Oh, I don't think—" I started to say but Emily cut me off.

"I do think that's a good idea." Emily nodded. "You guys can get everything out in the open."

"There's not much that we need to—" I said, but I was cut off once again.

"Oh, I disagree, Charlotte," Max said. "I think there is a lot we need to talk about." He nodded at Anabel, who stood up and then he grabbed my hand. "Why don't you come with me?"

"We can chat here." I stayed seated.

"I don't really think that this is the place you want us to have our conversation, is it?" He raised a single eyebrow at me. "Given our previous conversations and emails?"

"Well, uh ..." I looked at Anabel who seemed to be thinking. "What do you think?"

"It can't hurt to have a one-on-one conversation," she said after a few seconds and then she turned towards Max. "I hope you know that Charlotte had no ill intent or malice."

"Oh, I'm quite sure of that. She just wanted to benefit from my name." His voice was deceptively casual.

"Well, I wouldn't say *benefit*—" I started, but then I saw Anabel shoot a look at my Chanel handbag and I kept my mouth shut. "But of course I'd be willing to discuss this misunderstanding." I made an effort to sound friendly and nice. I wanted to tell Max Parker to take a long walk off of a short pier, but I knew that Anabel would wholly disapprove. "I am hungry though, so ..." My voice trailed off as I caught Max smiling about something. Our eyes met and for a few seconds, I forgot about what an arrogant asshole he was and just pictured him as a man. A very handsome man. A very handsome and rich man. It was a pity because under other circumstances, I would have quite liked to get to know him.

❦

*I'M EVER SO SORRY FOR LYING.* No, that's a big lie.

*I want you to know that I only lied the one time.* Yeah, right, he knew that wasn't true.

*How about we forget everything and you just put your tongue in my mouth. Or somewhere else.* I could feel myself blushing at that thought.

*Is it true what they say? Do you have a ten-inch cock?* I could feel my eyes going down to his lap and I snapped my head back up again as I felt his eyes on me. No way I was going to let him catch me checking out his goods.

Did I dare reach down and grab it? Just to check? *Yeah, right.* A giggle escaped before I could stop myself.

"Something funny?" Max finally spoke to me, his legs outstretched as he sat back.

"Nothing." I took a sip from the water bottle his driver had given me and looked around the back of the limo I now found myself in. I couldn't stop myself from squealing inside. I'd never been in a stretch limo before. Never had a chauffeur open a door for me and hand me a selection of snacks as I sat down. The plush leather seats were also more comfortable than my couch and I gawked at the full-size TV screen directly in front of us.

"So, Charlotte Johnson, I suppose you wonder why I wanted to talk?" Max look at me with a smug smile.

"Not really. I'm pretty sure I can guess why," I said with a shrug. "I have a reason for lying, you know. I'm not some weirdo; I didn't just pick your name out of a hat. This isn't something I go around doing."

"You mean you don't pretend to be dating a billionaire every month?" He cocked his head to the side. "What made me your lucky first?" He stressed the word *first,* and it made me blush.

"You're not my first." I stopped talking as I realized what I'd said. "I mean, you're the first guy I've ever said is my boyfriend that isn't. That is true. You're just not the first guy I've ever kissed or anything."

"I should hope not."

"You fired me," I said finally. "You bought my company, and you fired me, and I have no real savings, and I was mad, and well, things got out of hand. I didn't intend for this to happen."

"You didn't intend to lie?" He shifted closer to me in the backseat. "The lie just slipped out?"

"Yes."

"Funny that. I've never heard of a lie slipping out by mistake, or a cock slipping in by mistake, either."

"What?" I blushed at his words.

"You heard me." He shifted even closer to me and now his thigh was pressed against mine.

# THE BILLIONAIRE'S FAKE FIANCEE

"I didn't mean to lie. I was actually complaining about you when the hostess misheard me and—"

"Stop." He put his hand on my leg. "It doesn't matter now."

"Oh?" I pushed his hand off my thigh. "I hope you don't think I'm going to have sex with you because you caught me in a little white lie."

"Sex?" He laughed. "You think I'm driving you around for sex?"

"It certainly seems that way." I looked down at his legs so close to mine.

"Honey, I have a Rolodex two miles long. I don't need ..." He paused and looked me up and down, "or *want* you in that way."

I blushed at his remark. How rude was he? "Well, you certainly enjoyed kissing me," I spat back at him.

"Those pecks I gave you?" He laughed louder now. "Honey, my tongue didn't even enter your mouth. I've kissed dogs more passionately than I kissed you."

"Do you go around kissing dogs then?" I looked him up and down dismissively. "I suppose they're the only ones that could truly fancy a pompous asshole like you."

"There you go with the compliments again." He grabbed my hand. "I'm going to think that you can't get enough of me if you keep this up."

"What are you doing?" I swallowed hard as he ran a finger along my palm. "I thought you didn't want to sleep with me."

"Oh, I don't want you to sleep with me." He closed his fingers in on mine. "I need you to scratch an itch I didn't know I needed scratching."

"I'm not about to give you a blowjob." I shook my head vehemently. "I know you're some hotshot with a fancy limo and loads of money, but I'm not getting on my knees to you a blow job. No sir, I'm not some hooker."

"Hooker?" He threw his head back and laughed even louder. His hand let go of mine and he grabbed a bottle of water and chugged some down. "Oh, my dear, I don't think you're a hooker, and I don't want a blow job from you." He paused and looked at my lips. "Though I have to admit that if you begged me, I wouldn't say no."

"I would never beg to give you a blowjob."

"Well, you sure do like bringing it up, don't you?"

"I don't like bringing it up. I was just saying," I growled at him, flustered. "That's not an offer from me."

He leaned toward me. "What would you say if I dropped to the ground and put my head between your legs?" he whispered.

I blushed. Was he actually offering to go down on me? Was I dreaming? Would I dare?

"You're thinking too long, Charlotte. I'm not actually offering."

"I didn't think you were offering. I just wasn't about to answer such an obviously stupid question."

"Oh, of course." He nodded. "Of course."

"So what was it you wanted from me, then?" I asked him after about three minutes of silence. "And where are we going?"

"We're going to 727 5th Avenue."

"That means nothing to me." I sighed. "Is that where you live?"

"No." He shook his head. "I live in Chelsea."

"Oh. Okay."

"We're going to Tiffany's."

"Is that your girlfriend? The one I made mad at you?"

"What?" He blinked at me then as if he was confused. "Who?"

"Tiffany. The girl you just mentioned."

"Oh, no. We're going to Tiffany's. The jewelry store."

"We are? Why?" I licked my lips nervously. Was he playing with me? Was he actually trying to kidnap me? Why had I gotten into this limo with him again?

"To get you a ring."

"A ring?"

"Do you have a stutter?"

"No, I'm just very confused."

"Aww, I see." He nodded. "As confused as I was to hear that I had a girlfriend?"

"Touché." I rolled my eyes. "Am I never going to hear the end of this?"

"You will, but right now you owe me."

"I don't owe you anything. In fact, you owe me for making me lose my job."

"I need you to pretend to be my fake fiancée."

"You what?" I made a face. "Isn't that sentence redundant? Why would you say pretend and fake in the same sentence?"

"I didn't know you were an English major, Charlotte."

"Actually, I studied history at Columbia, so I'm not exactly a dumb blonde."

"I should think not. Your hair is brown."

"You know what I mean." I shook my head and sat back as questions raced in my mind. What had he meant that he wanted me to pretend to be his fiancée? Was that another way of saying he wanted me in his bed? Hadn't he just said that he didn't want to have sex with me?

"I need you to pretend to be my fiancée." He spoke more slowly this time. "It will help me out."

"How will it help you out?" I frowned. "I'm confused."

"I have a business deal. A very important business deal. With a Japanese company. Turns out they were very much in favor of doing business with a family man. A bachelor? Not so much ..." His voice trailed off. "I think you know what I'm saying."

"No, not really." I shook my head.

"I've been trying to do a billion-dollar deal with a company in Japan for two years. They have not been very responsive. All of a sudden they hear that I might be getting married, and they are interested in chatting." He paused. "I need to stay engaged for the time being."

"What would they care? Sounds like a bunch of bullshit to me."

"The company is a toy factory. They produce most of the toys manufactured in the world." He shrugged. "I guess they care who buys it."

I stared at him. "I don't owe you anything. You haven't even apologized for getting me fired."

"Sorry, Charlotte."

"That didn't sound the least bit sincere."

"I'm so, so sorry, Charlotte. Please forgive me."

His words mocked me, but I could tell from his tone that this was actually quite a sincere apology. He wanted me to forgive him. He wanted me to say yes. But why? Just so I could play his fake fiancée? What did he care? He could hire anyone to be his fiancée. Shit, he could easily get a real fiancée. He was hot as hell.

"I don't understand why you want or need me," I said honestly. "Like, look, I know what I did was wrong, and at the end of the day, I'm ashamed of my lies, but you don't really need me. I mean, you can sue me for libel or whatever, but I don't even have a pot to piss in, you won't get any money from me."

"You don't even have a pot?" His tone was sarcastic and I rolled my eyes.

"You know what I mean. It's just a saying."

"I like the fact that you're honest." He chuckled. "Which is ironic because you're actually a big liar. But you know the score. The other women in my life, well, let's just say that things would be complicated if I asked any of them to pretend to be my fiancée."

"How many of them are there?"

"Wouldn't you like to know?"

"That's why I asked." I ignored the ripple of jealousy that coursed through me. What did I think? He was a monk? He was gorgeous and rich. He was most probably sleeping with half of Manhattan.

"Look, my personal life is none of your business. This deal will be a transaction between you and me." He tapped his long fingers against the seat. "I just need you to play a part. You'll be well compensated, of course."

"I don't care about money." I held my head up high. "I know you might not believe that, but I'm not some sort of gold-digger. I'm not just all about money."

"I will compensate you for your time."

I paused. I wanted to tell him I didn't need to be compensated, but who was I kidding? I wasn't going to do this for free. He wasn't my best friend or my actual lover. If he wanted my help, he could pay.

"Oh, yeah? How much were you thinking?" I tried to sound nonchalant, but I needed to know if it would cover my rent.

"A fair amount." There was a sparkle in his eyes as if he knew that I wanted actual figures.

"Yeah, like how much are we talking?"

"I thought you didn't care about money?"

"I don't, but every job deserves to be paid fairly." I played with my fingers. I wondered if he'd be willing to give me an advance. "Also, how long will the job be lasting?"

"That I don't know." He shrugged. "It will last until the documents have all been signed and ratified."

"Then you'll dump me." I rolled my eyes. "Figured you wouldn't care once the contract was signed."

"What does that mean?" He looked at me sharply. "You really do have a low opinion of me, don't you?"

"Well, you bought Sally's company and told her you were going to keep us all on, and then you fired us."

"Sorry, I have no idea who Sally is."

I was incredulous. "You bought her graphics design company last month. I mean, I get it, you're rich, but do you really buy that many companies that you can't remember?"

"Yes, I really do buy that many companies. I'm in the business of buying and restructuring, Charlotte. Surely, your research gave you that much information about me." Then he looked at me with an amused look. "Or perhaps not. It doesn't seem like you did much research, did you? You didn't even know who I was."

I shrugged. "Google didn't have many photos of you."

"You said you were a history major? At Columbia?" He sounded disbelieving. "And yet, the only research you did was a Google search."

"Well, what would you have me do? Look you up in the library?" I said in my most surly tone, but I knew that any good researcher worth her salt would have done a far more exhaustive search.

"Did you *graduate* from Columbia?" He chuckled, and I rolled my eyes.

"So, my salary?" I prompted, needing to know an actual dollar amount.

"I was thinking I could pay you in kind, seeing as you said you're not interested in money."

"Pay me in kind? What the hell does that mean?"

"With kisses and sexually exciting adventures," he said with a straight face.

My jaw dropped. "You what?" My eyes narrowed at him. "You already told me you don't want me sexually."

"Can't a man change his mind?" He draped his arm around

my shoulder and played with my hair. "I think I'd quite like to see you bouncing up and down on—"

"That's enough!" I said, my face red. "That is not appropriate."

"Ten grand a week. How does that sound?" His fingers were still in my hair.

"Ten *thousand* dollars? US? A week?" I said, my voice squeaking. I was trying to keep my excitement down.

"Is that not enough?" He frowned. "Fifteen thousand dollars a week, with a minimum commitment of eight weeks? I think I should be able to get this deal done in four weeks. The next four weeks can be for us to wind down the relationship so that it looks like it was real."

"So, a hundred and twenty grand?" I wanted to sing and dance in the backseat.

"Yes, I'll give you half up-front and half at the end." He raised an eyebrow. "Does that work?"

"I suppose so." I grinned at him. "Am I going to get a check today?"

"Today?" He laughed. "You're an eager beaver, aren't you?"

"Well, I have bills to pay." I shrugged. "You know how it is."

"Yes, yes, I do." He looked at me thoughtfully. "You know I do quite like you, Charlotte Johnson. You have no pretenses about you. No games. Yes, I think you'll do quite nicely."

"I'm still not going to give you a blow job, you know. That will be a hundred grand extra." I grinned at my joke, but his expression didn't change. I quickly clarified. "That was a joke, by the way. Like I said before I'm no hooker, you can't pay me for sex or anything. I can't be bought."

"Good, good." He beamed. "Aww, we've arrived. Ready to pick out your ring?"

"Sure," I said as I looked out the window. We were in front of Tiffany's and the signature mint green awnings seemed to be calling out to me. "Let's go and get me a ring." The chauffeur opened the door for me then and I started to get out of the limo.

"Oh, and Charlotte?" Max said I made my way out.

"Yes?" I looked back at him.

"I never pay for it, but anytime, you want to drop on your knees and put those luscious lips around my cock, just let me know. I'll make the time to blow your world for free."

My jaw dropped at his words, but I didn't have time to respond because he was already getting out of the other side of the limo. I didn't know what to think or say. This man confused me. Did he want me or not? And more importantly, did I want him? It had been so long since I'd been with a man who excited me, but was it worth it to become involved with him? I already felt like I was in some sort of alternate reality. I didn't really know what to say or do, but I knew I could suck it up and play his fake fiancée for the next two months for $120 grand. That would take care of all my money woes for the time being and then maybe in the new year I could become an actress full time. And if he gave me an advance, I'd still have time to buy the gifts to mail overseas. I bit down on my lower lip as I walked into Tiffany's with Max behind me. This wasn't how it was meant to be. This wasn't how I was supposed to get my first engagement ring, but I supposed it didn't matter now. My daydreams of finding true love had blown up on the day that Brandon had gone.

CHAPTER 8

"So, then the guy said, 'So we're set on the 2.06 carat diamond and the platinum setting'?" I recounted my afternoon's shopping trip to Emily. "And then Max was like, 'Well you said that's the biggest diamond you have in stock, right?'" I giggled as I held my hand up for her to admire. "And, well, that's basically the whole story. What do you think?"

"Whoa. Could that diamond be any bigger?" She grinned at me. "Are you trying to blind me?"

"Haha, can you believe it?" I sipped from my iced mocha and then looked at my phone screen. "Ugh, I only have thirty minutes left before Max and the limo come back to pick me up."

"I just can't keep up with you." Emily shook her head. "I have no idea how this happened. I thought he was going to take you straight to the police station."

"What?" My jaw dropped. "So why did you encourage me to go with him, then?"

"Well, I mean it was either the police station or his bedroom for some bow chicka bow wow," she said with a laugh. "It was worth the risk. He's hot, and you need to get laid."

"Emily!" I rolled my eyes at her. "This is a *business* agreement. There is not going to be any sex."

"Pull the other one, Charlotte. Maybe Anabel will believe that shit, but you want him badly." She leaned back in her seat. "And if for some reason you don't want him, I'll have him. Shit, I haven't had a date in over a year. I'd be happy to bang one out with him."

"Emily, you're worse than a guy, you know that right?"

"Not possible." She shook her head. "So do I get a shot with him or ...?"

"I'm not even answering that question. Don't you think I'm already in enough trouble?"

"Yeah, but that's you, not me."

"Haha."

"You know I'm just joking. So he's coming to pick you up and then you're going to go back to your place?"

"To *pack* because then we're catching a plane and going overseas." I couldn't hold in my excitement. "He has a private jet, but we're flying commercial because he's trying to watch his carbon footprint."

"As he should."

"But we're flying first class!!"

"To Japan?"

"No," I shook my head. "I think he said we're going to Australia."

"Australia?"

"Yeah. I can't remember why, though."

"I thought the deal he was trying to close was in Japan though?"

"It is."

"So why Australia?"

"Girl, who knows and who cares?"

"True, so have you signed the contract yet?"

"No, he's getting it written up now." I licked my lips nervously. "I kinda have my own requirements I want to add, but I'm not sure if I should bring them up to him."

"Oh?" Emily looked surprised. "What are your requirements?"

"I don't want him to think I'll be at his beck and call every minute of the day." I took a deep breath. "And I just want him to respect me."

"Oh, that's nothing." Emily smiled at me. "You're doing him a favor. Of course he'll respect you."

"I don't know. I think he thinks this is all fun and games for me. And I mean, why wouldn't it be, right? For most women, it would be the opportunity of a lifetime."

"But you're not most women."

"He doesn't know that." I exhaled and then put my face in my hands and tried to suppress all the nervous thoughts that were threatening to take control of my body. I hadn't felt this level of anxiety in years. Was I making a mistake?

"Do you think I'm a bad person?" I said, all of a sudden serious. "I'm selling my soul, in a way."

"You're not a bad person, Char." Emily leaned forward and squeezed my hand. "You know that, right? You're not the one who made this plan. It was Max."

"But I'm doing it for money." I pursed my lips. "Maybe I should just go home. My parents miss me." I knew they would be delighted to see me. It had been years since I'd been home. I FaceTimed them every week, but that wasn't the same.

"You can't move back home." Emily shook her head. "I won't let you. I'd miss you too much."

"But this doesn't feel like a good idea anymore." I stared at the ring in my hand. "This is fake. It means nothing. I don't want to be this person, driven by money. I should go home, but I can't. The memories ..." My voice trailed off. "It still hurts, Em. It still hurts." I could feel tears welling in my eyes and I took a deep breath.

"I know." She nodded and this time she squeezed my hand a little tighter. "He was your everything."

"When we were young, I talked so much about getting engaged. About wearing a ring on this finger. I showed him so many rings that he most probably never wanted to see another engagement ring in his life." I half cried, half laughed. "And now here I am with a ring and it's gorgeous, and it means nothing. I shouldn't be doing this."

"You can't live in the past, Charlotte." Emily took a deep breath. "Brandon wouldn't ..." she paused as she realized the effect her saying his name had on me. "I'm sorry. I know that this isn't how you planned your engagement to go."

"I guess it's what I deserve." I tried to smile. "It's funny how life goes, eh? You try and keep a big smile on your face. You try and stay positive, but it still shits on you when you're not paying attention."

"If you don't want to do this, then you don't have to," Emily said. "I have some money I can lend you."

"You what? But you're as broke as me."

"I have a rainy day fund," she explained. "After growing up the way I did." She had a faraway look on her face. "It's important to me to have a backup fund, just in case."

"I never knew."

"It's literally for emergencies and emergencies only. I have about ten grand."

"Wow, that's amazing." I was so impressed by my friend and disgusted with myself for having nothing. "You can't lend that to me, Emily. That's your emergency fund."

"I don't want you to feel like you have to do something you don't want to do for money. Friends don't let that happen.

Family doesn't let that happen," she said seriously. "It's yours if you want it."

"No, I'll be fine. The past is the past." I finished the last of my iced mocha and clenched my fists. "I just need to be more responsible. Like you."

"Don't get carried away, now," she said with a small laugh. "So, do you think you'll have to make out with Max or anything?"

"I don't know." I tried to ignore the butterflies in my stomach as I thought about getting down and dirty with Max. "We shall see."

"It's okay to have fun, you know," Emily said softly. "It's okay to enjoy being with someone else."

"I just never thought I'd be here, in a position like this." I let out a deep sigh. "He was my Brandon."

"Things should have been different, Char." She nodded. "But he made the choice. You have to remember that. He made the choice. Not you."

"I know." I let out a bitter laugh. "A part of me wishes I'd begged him not to go."

"I know." She sighed as well. "But we both know that wouldn't have stopped him."

"It would be all about sex with Max." I could feel myself going red. "I'm definitely attracted to him. I can't lie, but is it bad that all I want him for is sex? I mean, not that I want him for sex, but I have to admit it has crossed my mind."

"Girl, men have used women for centuries to get what they want. Don't think too much about it." Her voice was no-nonsense now. "You get yours."

"Yeah, true." I laughed and then I heard my phone beeping. "That's weird. I thought I put my ringer on silent." I pulled the phone out of my handbag. "It's Max. He texted me."

"Ooh, what did he say?"

I pressed open on the text and read aloud. "Check your email." I rolled my eyes. "He's such a bossyboots. I can't stand it."

"What does his email say?" Emily looked intrigued.

"Let me see." I clicked on my inbox icon. There were three missed emails from Max.

I opened the first one curious as to what he was sending me.

To: ArtyCharlotteJohnson@Gmail.com
From: MaxParkerCEO@Parkercorporation.com
Subject: Unmentionables

Dear Charlotte,

I hope you are enjoying coffee with your friend. I'm having your contract drawn up as we speak and was wondering what size bra you wore?

Max

To: ArtyCharlotteJohnson@Gmail.com
From: MaxParkerCEO@Parkercorporation.com
Re: Unmentionables


Dear Charlotte,

I don't want to take liberties, but if I had to guess I'd say you were a 36C? More than a bite, but slightly less than a handful.

Max

To: ArtyCharlotteJohnson@Gmail.com
From: MaxParkerCEO@Parkercorporation.com
Re: Unmentionables

THE BILLIONAIRE'S FAKE FIANCEE

Dear Charlotte,
Do you prefer thongs or bikini briefs?
Max

I stared at the emails in shock, not knowing if he was joking around or what? Surely, he didn't expect me to answer that question? I passed my phone over to Emily who started laughing as soon as she read them.

"Well, I guess we know that he's not interested in just a platonic relationship."

"He's crazy." I shook my head. "I'm not responding to these emails."

"What are you going to do?"

"Nothing." I glared at my phone screen. "I asked him in the limo if he was expecting to have sex, and he made it seem as if that was the furthest thing from his mind."

"And you believed him?"

"Well, I mean ..." I just grinned at her. "Really, who could resist me?"

"Respond to him! Go on!"

"What should I say?"

"He thinks you're a prude and that he's shocking you," Emily said. "Girl, he thinks he's got you all hot and bothered. Spin it around on him."

"How?"

"Go even further." She grinned. "He won't know what the hell to do with himself."

"You're right." I sat up straight and laughed. "I might as well have some fun with it, right?"

"Right. We're twenty-five. If ever there was a time for us to just let loose and have some fun, then this is it."

"True, true. Okay, I'm going to email back.

*To: MaxParkerCEO@Parkercorporation.com*

*From: ArtyCharlotteJohnson@Gmail.com*
Re: Unmentionables

Dear Max,

I rarely wear panties. So I don't prefer thongs or bikini briefs. Sometimes I do wear boyfriend shorts, but usually that's after a night of passionate lovemaking. As to my bra size, good guess, but not quite. I guess you're not as familiar with ladies' breasts as you thought. I wear a 36D bra. May I ask you why you want to know?
Charlotte

To: ArtyCharlotteJohnson@Gmail.com
From: MaxParkerCEO@Parkercorporation.com
Re: Unmentionables

Dear Charlotte,
Are you wearing no panties right now?
Max

*To: MaxParkerCEO@Parkercorporation.com*
*From: ArtyCharlotteJohnson@Gmail.com*
Re: Unmentionables

Dear Max,
How can I be wearing no panties?
Charlotte

To: ArtyCharlotteJohnson@Gmail.com
From: MaxParkerCEO@Parkercorporation.com
Re: Unmentionables

Dear Charlotte,

I'm picking you up at the coffee shop in five minutes. I can check for myself.
Max

*To: MaxParkerCEO@Parkercorporation.com*
*From: ArtyCharlotteJohnson@Gmail.com*
Re: Unmentionables

Dear Max,
You wish.
Charlotte

To: ArtyCharlotteJohnson@Gmail.com
From: MaxParkerCEO@Parkercorporation.com
Re: Unmentionables

Dear Charlotte,
You have no idea what I'm wishing.
Max

*To: MaxParkerCEO@Parkercorporation.com*
*From: ArtyCharlotteJohnson@Gmail.com*
Re: Unmentionables

Dear Max,
I think I do.
Charlotte

To: ArtyCharlotteJohnson@Gmail.com
From: MaxParkerCEO@Parkercorporation.com
Re: Unmentionables

Dear Charlotte,

I have the contract ready, but there are some amendments I'd like to make. If you're up for it.
Hard Max

*To: MaxParkerCEO@Parkercorporation.com*
*From: ArtyCharlotteJohnson@Gmail.com*
Re: Unmentionables

Dear Mad Max,
I'm always up for it, I just don't know if I'm up for you.
Charlotte

To: ArtyCharlotteJohnson@Gmail.com
From: MaxParkerCEO@Parkercorporation.com
Re: Unmentionables

Dear Charlotte,
I'm up for you, so that's all the matters.
Up and Ready

*To: MaxParkerCEO@Parkercorporation.com*
*From: ArtyCharlotteJohnson@Gmail.com*
Re: Unmentionables

Dear Stone,
You'd be lucky. I've got a vibrator that can do the job better than any man.
Charlotte

To: ArtyCharlotteJohnson@Gmail.com
From: MaxParkerCEO@Parkercorporation.com
Re: Unmentionables

Sit on my face and see if my tongue isn't better than your vibrator.

*To: MaxParkerCEO@Parkercorporation.com*
*From: ArtyCharlotteJohnson@Gmail.com*
Re: Unmentionables

No comment.

To: ArtyCharlotteJohnson@Gmail.com
From: MaxParkerCEO@Parkercorporation.com
Re: Unmentionables

I'm outside. Bring your friend. We can drop her off at home.

*To: MaxParkerCEO@Parkercorporation.com*
*From: ArtyCharlotteJohnson@Gmail.com*
Re: Unmentionables

I'll be right there.

## CHAPTER 9

"So, are you ready to sign it?" Max motioned to the paperwork on his desk, and I shook my head.

"I need to go home." I looked at my phone and yawned. "I'm tired. It's been a long day, and I need to think everything through."

"You're not having second thoughts, are you?" He looked up quickly, an unusual expression on his face, almost like fear. Why would he be scared that I was going to leave? That made no sense.

"I just need to process everything." I pursed my lips. "I'll still play my part. I just need to figure out what my boundaries are."

"What your boundaries are?" He got up from his chair and walked towards me. "What do you mean, you need to figure out what your boundaries are?"

"We're flirting, and while it's all in good fun, I want to decide if I want to go there with you. There are many men out there, and well, I don't know if I want to waste time with you."

"Waste time with me?" His lips twitched. "You don't think I'd be a good lover?"

"I don't like to mix business with pleasure."

"What if I do?"

"What if you do what?" I feigned ignorance, and he chuckled as he stood next to my chair.

"What if I want to kiss you?" He dropped to his knees and kissed the side of my cheek. "Here." He kissed my nose. "And here." He kissed my forehead. "And here." He kissed me on the lips and stared into my eyes. "And here," he murmured against my lips, and I felt his hand behind my head, playing with my hair as his tongue entered my mouth smoothly.

I kissed him back, enjoying the taste of coffee on his lips. His right hand found its way to my leg and he ran his fingers along my thigh. I was glad that I was wearing leggings so that he didn't have easy access to slip under my skirt. I moaned as he bit down on my lower lip and then pulled away from me. "I take it that was acceptable?"

"Mhmm." I didn't really know how to answer that. I didn't want to lie. It had been more than acceptable. His lips had tasted like manna. His touch had felt like warmth on a cold day. I craved more of him, needed more of him. I looked at his face and into his eyes and tried to read his expression. His eyebrows were furrowed as he gazed at me, his blue eyes dark with desire, his dark hair complimenting his olive tan and his perfect white teeth completing his look of perfection.

"You remind me of a young Tom Selleck." I gazed at him. "When he was in *Magnum PI*."

"You know *Magnum PI*?" He looked surprised. "You seem a bit young to have watched that."

"I'm twenty-five," I said. "How old are you?"

"Thirty." He grinned. "Most people only know him from *Friends*."

"I loved him in *Friends*." I grinned. "You look older than thirty."

"Well, thanks." He grimaced. "Glad to know I look old."

"You don't look *old*—" I said hastily and stopped as he started laughing. "Oh good, you're not upset at me."

"How could I be upset at you? You told me I look like Magnum PI."

"You know the show?"

"Yeah, my best friend loved it." He nodded. "How do you know it?"

"My family watched it all the time when I was growing up. My mom had a crush on Tom Selleck when she was younger, and we had the videos and then later the DVD collection."

"Aww," he smiled. "Makes sense."

"We used to watch it as a family every Friday night." I smiled as I thought back to my childhood. "Friday nights we'd watch *Magnum PI*, then on Saturday we'd go to the beach and possibly the mall, and then on Sunday, we'd go to church. Every single weekend was the same routine," I said in a soft voice. "Until I was thirteen."

"What happened when you were thirteen?" He looked at me curiously.

"Everything changed," I said, and then, because I didn't want to talk about my childhood anymore, I stood up. "You have a nice office." I walked to the window behind his desk. "This is an awesome view." I looked out and down Broadway and smiled as I watched the hundreds of people walking up and down the street. "I thought you'd have your office off of Wall Street or something."

"I'm not the typical CEO." He came and stood next to me. "As my fiancée, I thought you would have figured that out already."

"Yeah," I said as I looked at the photos he had by his bookshelf. There were no personal photos of him and other family members. No photos of him with any women. No photos with him and any friends, either. There was a photo of him holding a $20 bill and another of him with a golden retriever dog. Next to the photos, there was a degree from Harvard Business School and next to that there was a photo of a man in an Army uniform.

I looked at the photo and then turned to him. "Is that your dad?" I pointed to the photo.

"No." He shook his head and then held up the photo next to his face. "It's me."

"You were in the Army?" I was surprised. Rich boys didn't join the military. They didn't have to.

"Yeah, for three years." He stared into my eyes searching for something. I suddenly felt uncomfortable in his presence. What was he looking for?

"But you went to college and business school?" I was confused. "When did you enlist?"

"During college." He looked away from me then. "I had some demons I needed to face. It made me a better man. A stronger man."

"Did you need the GI Bill for your tuition?" I asked him hesitantly.

"No." He shook his head, but he didn't say anything else.

"Where were you stationed?"

"Bagram Air Base. Afghanistan."

"Oh." I felt cold again as I stared at him. Afghanistan was a dangerous place. A deadly place. "I'm glad you made it back safely."

"Thank you," he said and then he put the photo down. "Would you like some water or a glass of wine?"

"I'm okay, thanks." I shook my head and made my way back to the chair in front of his desk and took a seat.

"I made a mistake earlier." He came and sat on the desk in

front of me. I looked up at him in confusion. What was he talking about?

"What mistake did you make?"

"I said your hair was brown, but it's not brown, is it? It's black."

"Oh," I laughed as I touched my hair self-consciously. "It's a very dark brown, but yeah, pretty much black."

"Raven-haired." He smiled and then looked away for a few seconds, muttering something under his breath.

"Sorry, I can't hear you clearly."

"Oh, that's my fault. Your hair color reminded me of my favorite poem."

"Oh? What poem is that?"

"'The Raven,' by Edgar Allan Poe. Do you know it?"

"Not really. I think I read it once in high school English class, though." I shrugged. "Perhaps, I can't really remember."

"Once Upon a Midnight Dreary," he said with a small smile. "That's how it starts."

"I know that one song by Blues Traveler, what was it called again? 'Run Around'?" I said. "I think the first line is the same."

"I think you're right." He grinned and then grabbed his phone. "Let's check and see." I watched as he pressed some buttons on his phone and then the song started playing through his phone speaker. "That's cool." He looked at me appreciatively. "I'm impressed."

"Well, I'd be impressed if you can quote me some more of 'The Raven.'"

"Okay, then. Hold on, let me think."

I watched as he closed his eyes for a few seconds. And then he opened his eyes again and stood up, throwing his hands up into the air and grinning.

"But the Raven, sitting lonely on the placid bust, spoke only
That one word, as if his soul in that one word he did outpour.
Nothing further then he uttered—not a feather then he fluttered—
Till I scarcely more than muttered "Other friends have flown before—
On the morrow *he* will leave me, as my hopes have flown before.
Then the bird said, 'Nevermore.'"

He stopped then and took a little bow as I clapped for him. He grabbed my hands and pulled me up off of the chair.

"I feel like I've known you forever, Charlotte Johnson," he said as he gazed at me. I held my breath as I waited for him to kiss me again. I could almost taste his lips on mine again. I was going to run my hands through his hair this time. I wanted to see if it felt as silky as it looked. But instead of kissing me, he took a step back.

"Shall I call you a car, then?" He looked at his watch. "I can hand you these papers, and you can take them home and read them through, and we can reconvene tomorrow."

"You didn't tell me what amendments you wanted to make," I said. I felt like I'd just been rejected, even though I hadn't asked him for anything.

"I changed my mind." He was pressing buttons on his phone now. "No need to make any amendments." He looked up then and nodded. "The contract as it stands is fine."

"I see."

I grabbed the papers from his desk. He was hiding something, but I didn't know what. What were the amendments that he'd wanted to make? And why had he changed his mind?

"Are you calling the car?" I asked him as he held the phone to his head. He shook his head and put his finger to his lips.

"Hey, Sandy, it's me, Max. What are you up to?" He chuckled. "That's what I thought. Why don't you drop by my place tonight?" He looked at me then, and I could feel my entire body shaking as my soul sunk into the ground. Was he really going to play this game?

If there was one thing I didn't do, it was games. And men who wanted other women.

I turned around and headed to the door as he was still talking and I had my hand on the doorknob when I felt his hand on my shoulder.

"Where do you think you're going?"

"Home." I looked over my shoulder and tried to keep my face impassive. I didn't want him to know I was jealous and pissed off. "Like I said before."

"My driver isn't here yet," he said. He glared at me, the phone still attached to his ear.

"That's your problem, not mine." I pulled my hand back. "Have fun with your little friend and just email me later."

"You're not leaving." He pushed his body against the door. "We're not done."

"I think we are, Max." I pushed his chest, my hands loving the feel of his rock hard body. "You're not my jailer. I'm leaving."

"Charlotte." His tone was light but threatening.

"*Max*," I said in the same tone. And then I leaned forward and placed my lips next to his ear. "Max Parker, get your body off of the door ..." I blew into his ear then and I ran my right hand down his chest all the way to his pants and lightly down his crotch. He was hard, and I swallowed. He was as turned on as I was. That made me smile slightly, but I wasn't going to let him know.

"Move," I said and pushed him. He fell back, a dazed look on his face. "I'm going to catch the subway and head home. Email me."

Before he could react, I opened the door and headed out of his office. I looked back from the hallway and I could see him watching me with veiled eyes, looking taken aback and bewildered. I turned back around and looked for the elevator so that I could leave, a small smile on my face.

Score: Charlotte 1, Max 0.

## CHAPTER 10

To: ArtyCharlotteJohnson@Gmail.com
From: MaxParkerCEO@Parkercorporation.com
Subject: Tonight

CHARLOTTE,
I will be at your apartment at 7 p.m. to talk.
Max

*To: MaxParkerCEO@Parkercorporation.com*
*From: ArtyCharlotteJohnson@Gmail.com*
Re: Tonight

I WON'T BE HERE.

TO: ARTYCHARLOTTEJOHNSON@GMAIL.COM

From: MaxParkerCEO@Parkercorporation.com
Re: Tonight

CHARLOTTE,

Where will you be? You didn't say you had other plans. You can see your friends tomorrow. Tonight we need to chat.

Max

*To: MaxParkerCEO@Parkercorporation.com*
*From: ArtyCharlotteJohnson@Gmail.com*
Re: Tonight

DEAR BOSSYBOOTS,

I love that you assume that the only people I could have plans with are my friends. I have a hot date coming over. I think you know what for, or do I have to spell it out for you? Let's just say my panties are wet just thinking about it. I will see you tomorrow.

Charlotte "in for a good time tonight" Johnson

TO: ARTYCHARLOTTEJOHNSON@GMAIL.COM
From: MaxParkerCEO@Parkercorporation.com
Re: Tonight

DEAR CAN YOUR PANTIES BE WET IF YOU DON'T WEAR THEM,

Bullshit. I'll be over in thirty minutes.

Max, your de facto boss

*To: MaxParkerCEO@Parkercorporation.com*
*From: ArtyCharlotteJohnson@Gmail.com*
Re: Tonight

Dear Charlotte,

How many women can you have in one night?

Do not, and I repeat, DO NOT come over to my house tonight.

Charlotte "Do crotchless panties count as panties" Johnson

To: ArtyCharlotteJohnson@Gmail.com
From: MaxParkerCEO@Parkercorporation.com
Re: Tonight

Are you trying to make me hard?

*To: MaxParkerCEO@Parkercorporation.com*
*From: ArtyCharlotteJohnson@Gmail.com*
Re: Tonight

It doesn't seem that hard. Pun intended.

To: ArtyCharlotteJohnson@Gmail.com
From: MaxParkerCEO@Parkercorporation.com
Re: Tonight

I need to put you across my lap and spank you.

To: MaxParkerCEO@Parkercorporation.com
From: ArtyCharlotteJohnson@Gmail.com
Re: Tonight

Figures you would be into that kinky shit. Next thing you'll be wanting to gag me and use handcuffs.

To: ArtyCharlotteJohnson@Gmail.com
From: MaxParkerCEO@Parkercorporation.com
Re: Tonight

Don't tempt me. I'd love to gag you. And then slap that pert bottom of yours. I'll be there in fifteen minutes.

To: MaxParkerCEO@Parkercorporation.com
From: ArtyCharlotteJohnson@Gmail.com
Re: Tonight

I told you not to come over. What if I wanted to slap that rock hard butt of yours?

To: ArtyCharlotteJohnson@Gmail.com
From: MaxParkerCEO@Parkercorporation.com

Re: Tonight

ANOTHER BODY PART OF MINE IS ROCK HARD RIGHT NOW. Want a photo?

*To: MaxParkerCEO@Parkercorporation.com*
*From: ArtyCharlotteJohnson@Gmail.com*
Re: Tonight

NO THANKS. I'VE SEEN ENOUGH PENCILS IN MY LIFE.

To: ArtyCharlotteJohnson@Gmail.com
From: MaxParkerCEO@Parkercorporation.com
Re: Tonight

THAT SOUNDS LIKE A CHALLENGE. THREE MINUTES AWAY.

*To: MaxParkerCEO@Parkercorporation.com*
*From: ArtyCharlotteJohnson@Gmail.com*
Re: Tonight

NOT A GOOD IDEA FOR YOU TO COME OVER RIGHT NOW. Also, why don't you text like a regular human being?

To: ArtyCharlotteJohnson@Gmail.com
From: MaxParkerCEO@Parkercorporation.com

Re: Tonight

IS THAT YOUR WAY OF ASKING FOR A DICK PIC?

*To: MaxParkerCEO@Parkercorporation.com*
*From: ArtyCharlotteJohnson@Gmail.com*
Re: Tonight

BYE, MAX. I WILL SEE YOU TOMORROW.

I ROLLED MY EYES AS I CLOSED OUT OF MY EMAIL. I LEANED back on my couch and rubbed my eyes. I was feeling a little hot and bothered after that exchange. Okay, if I'm being honest, I was feeling a *lot* hot and bothered. Max had a way of getting under my skin that no man ever had before in my life.

Was he really coming over? It made no sense for him to come over, especially if he'd arranged for someone else to go over to his place that night. He was just trying to get a rise out of me, I was almost positive. I knew men well enough to know that they loved to egg women on. I could remember Brandon doing that to me all the time. Trying to trick me into being upset with him, so that he could surprise me and make me happy. Like that time when he'd pretended he'd forgotten my birthday and then I found out he'd gotten me a copy of the Articles of Confederation as a present. I'd been so sad and then so happy.

"I'd never forget, Charlotte," he'd whispered into my ear before giving me a big hug. "You know that." He'd brushed my hair back and smiled at me with such love that I'd just grinned back at him. I had been closer to him than anyone else in my life, and even though he'd been five years older than me, we'd never really noticed the age difference. When we were together, we were just us.

I jumped up and walked over to my bookshelf and looked through my books for the copy of *Huckleberry Finn* that he'd given me. I opened it to the title page and read the quote he'd taken from the book and written down:

TO MY LOVE CHAR BEAR,

"What's the use you learning to do right when it's troublesome to do right and ain't no trouble to do wrong, and the wages is just the same?"- Live your life to its fullest potential and don't let anything hold you back.

Love Always,
Brandon XOXO


"OH, BRANDON," I HELD THE BOOK TO MY HEART AS TEARS threatened to fall. Why was it still so hard? Why was he always on my mind? I missed him. I missed being with him. Even though he'd lied to me. Even though he'd left me. I still remembered the good times and I still wished things were different.

*Beep beep.*

Someone was texting me. I walked back over to the couch, placed the book on the coffee table, and grabbed my phone.


MAX: YOU DIDN'T ANSWER MY LAST EMAIL, SO I ASSUME YOU *want to text instead.*
*Charlotte: Max, I told you I'm busy.*
*Max: Do you want that photo from me?*

*Charlotte: Send it.*

*Max: What?*

*Charlotte: That's what I thought. All talk and no show.*

*Max: Here you go... {click to view attachment}*

*Charlotte: That's your face...not your cock.*

*Max: Show me your breasts first.*

*Charlotte: I'm not showing you anything. You're the one who offered me a pic.*

*Max: Ok, here you go... {click to view attachment}*

*Charlotte: Whoa, you nearly had me for a second, that's your thumb.*

*Max: Haha, smart girl. I thought that would have fooled ya.*

*Charlotte: I wasn't born yesterday.*

*Max: I'm outside your door.*

*Charlotte: What?*

*Max: I'm outside your door. Open up.*

*Charlotte: You didn't knock.*

*Max: I didn't want to scare you.*

*Charlotte: Max, I told you that this wasn't a good time.*

*Max: I guess I'm calling your bluff.*

*Charlotte: Max.*

*Max: Open the God Damn door, Charlotte.*

*Charlotte: Fine. I'm coming.*

*Max: That's what she said.*

"You're so immature," I said as I opened the door. Max walked into my apartment, a huge grin on his face. "You're rude as well. I told you that I have plans tonight."

"Those plans will have to change." He looked around my small apartment. "Is this a studio?" I nodded and I watched as he made his way over to my window with the view of Central Park. "It's cute. Small, but cute."

"Is that what women say about you and your ..." My voice trailed off and I looked down at his pants.

"You wish." He threw his head back and laughed. "I don't get any complaints."

"I'm sure Sandy is excited."

"Sandy?" He said her name and then grinned. "Are you jealous?"

"Jealous of what?"

"My fuck buddy."

"Crude." I shook my head, but I knew my face was going red. "Would you like a drink?"

"Sure, I'll take a whiskey."

"I don't have whiskey."

"A gin and tonic?"

"Nope." I shook my head again.

"An IPA?"

"Nope."

"What do you have, then, Charlotte?"

"I have two apple ciders, a bottle of red wine, water, chocolate milk ... oh, and some ginger ale."

"I see." He paused. "I'm fine. Thanks."

"Is that the first time in the world those words have ever been spoken by you?" I stared at him with widened eyes, pretending to be shocked. "I'm sure many people haven't heard you say you were fine before."

"Is that what you're wearing on your supposed date?" He looked me up and down and I could see a sly smile on his face as he took in my oversized Columbia sweater and gym shorts. His eyes went down and stayed on the red and white striped socks I was wearing, and I could tell that he was trying not to laugh. Asshole.

"Anything wrong with my attire?" I held my head straight up in the air and looked at him through narrowed eyes.

"No, it's very sexy," he said with a smirk. "I know I'd be down to hook up with a woman in fox socks."

"Good to know." I walked over to him. "How can I help you, Max? What was so urgent that it couldn't wait until tomorrow?" I reached up and undid my ponytail and shook my hair down my back. I could see his eyes focus on my hair and then on my lips, and so I pulled off my sweater and threw it onto the couch. His eyes fell to my chest area now, and I heard a sudden intake of breath. I was wearing a loose-fitting white t-shirt with a V-neck and no bra underneath. I was pretty sure that he could see my hardened nipples poking through the top.

"I thought we should discuss what's expected of you in your role as my fiancée. And well I thought we could get to know each other better."

"Oh, I see." I placed my hand on his chest and slowly started undoing the buttons to his shirt. It was like some other being had taken over me, but I wanted to see his body. "Well, let's get this party started, then."

"I didn't mean in the Biblical sense," he said, though he didn't stop me from unbuttoning his shirt. "I meant we should learn about each other's personalities and all that good stuff." His breath caught as I pulled his shirt out of his jeans and stared at his naked chest. It was absolute perfection. His skin was a tanned golden brown with a light smattering of dark hair across his pecks. His six-pack was taut and smooth, and I ran my fingers across his skin. "Unless, of course, you had other ideas."

"No," I said quickly and pulled my hand back. "I was just curious." I licked my lips and walked back to the couch and sat down. "What do you want to know?"

"Can I pull your shirt off as well?" he asked as he followed me to the couch and sat next to me.

"What do you think?"

"I think it's unfair that you got to touch my stomach and I didn't get to touch yours."

"Well, we can fix that right now." I grabbed his hand and placed it under my shirt and on my stomach. I didn't have a six-pack, or abs at all, really, but I liked my body, even though I could have stood to lose about twenty pounds.

His fingers ran across my stomach and played with my belly button, and I enjoyed the warm, firm touch of his skin against mine. My hand dropped away as he moved his hand higher, closer to my breasts, my heart racing as his fingers traced up the valley between them. Our eyes connected, and I could see a question in his gaze. His hand stilled and he cocked his head to the side slightly. He wanted to know if it was okay to go further. I was momentarily surprised by that. But then I reached over and kissed him on the lips slightly and he grinned. His hands found my breasts, and he cupped them in his palms, squeezing my nipples and rubbing his palm against them roughly. I pushed him onto the couch and fell forward on top of him and he adjusted his body so that I was lying to the side of him. His right hand then ran back down my stomach towards my shorts and then inside of my shorts towards the top of my panties.

"Liar," he whispered as his fingers worked their way in between my legs and he rubbed gently on the material.

"What?" I said innocently as I ran my hands down his back.

"You are wearing panties, and they aren't crotchless." His voice was hoarse as his lips found the side of my neck and he rubbed against my clit. My fingers found their way to the front of his pants and I rubbed his hardness, smiling as I felt it twitching in his pants. His fingers then slipped into the side of my panties, and I felt him touching me softly. I moaned at the feel of him and arched my back, pressing my

# THE BILLIONAIRE'S FAKE FIANCEE

breasts against him. He groaned as I fumbled with his belt buckle and tried to undo his pants.

"You're wet for me, aren't you?" he whispered in my ear, the desire in his voice clear. I nodded and almost whined as he removed his finger from my panties and pulled my them off quickly. My breasts were now on display for him, and he whistled as he stared at my chest. He leaned down to take a nipple into his mouth and I cried out as I felt his teeth biting down lightly.

*Knock, knock!*

The sound of knocking on my door made us both jump.

"You weren't kidding?" His eyes narrowed as he stared at me in shock. I grabbed my shirt and pulled it back on quickly.

"Kidding about what?"

"You have another man coming over to fuck you?" He looked pissed off, and I almost laughed at his furious expression.

"No, I don't know—"

I walked towards my front door. I had absolutely no idea who was here. I wasn't expecting anyone, and I hadn't had sex in over a year, so there was certainly no booty call showing up to pleasure me. I readjusted my shirt and shorts and then opened the door.

"Charlotte, there you are!" Anabel beamed at me as she gave me a quick hug. "Emily told me she met you for coffee and that you were going to sign some crazy contract and I wanted to make sure you were okay because you haven't been answering your phone ..."

The sound of Max standing up alerted her to the fact that we weren't alone. Her gaze shifted and her eyes opened. "Oh," she said softly and looked back at me, a certain gleeful expression in her eyes. "Am I disturbing something?"

"No," I said quickly.

"Yes," Max said as he approached us. "Charlotte was just packing up some stuff so that she can come home with me tonight."

"What?" I said and blinked at him. "No, I'm not."

"It's going to make everything a lot easier if you stay at my place for the next two months," he said, his tone once again bossy. "You will have your own suite of rooms, don't worry about that."

"It's unreasonable for you to think that I can just come and stay with you," I said, annoyed. "Don't you think so, Anabel?"

"Well, I ... yes, in a way," she said with a slight nod. "Though, I suppose if you're to be a believable fiancée, you would live with him."

"Anabel!" I scolded her. "How can you take his side?"

"I'm just saying, is all." She shrugged and then grinned. "I should go. I didn't realize you guys were busy."

"We're not busy," I growled at her. "Come inside."

"Your t-shirt is not on properly." She giggled and gave me a quick hug. "Just have some fun and enjoy yourself. You deserve it." She leaned back. "Good seeing you, Max," she said with a small nod. "I hope we get to know each other better."

"I'm sure we will," he said with a small smile. "Good seeing you again, Anabel."

"You, too." She turned around and walked back out of the door. "Bye, guys." And with that she was gone.

I turned to Max to tell him off, but he was walking back to the couch and towards my bookshelf.

"You have a wide variety of books."

"I come from a family of readers." I nodded. "My dad loves sci-fi, my mom loves romance, and my brother loved classics."

"And you love them all."

"Yeah, you could say that." I walked towards him. "You can't change the subject, you know. I'm not coming to stay at your apartment."

"Penthouse suite."

"What?"

"I wouldn't say I live in an apartment. I'd say I live in a penthouse suite."

"Fine, Max. I'm not coming to stay in your penthouse suite."

"I think you'll find you will." He bent down and picked up the copy of *Huckleberry Finn* that was on my coffee table. "I loved this book as a boy. I can't believe they banned it from schools."

"Some schools banned *Harry Potter* as well," I said with a shrug. "Can't let schools dictate what you read."

"Are you reading it now?"

"No." I shook my head. "I was just looking at it. To ... see something."

"Cool, cool." He placed the book back down on the table and looked at the maps over my living room couch. "These are, uhm, interesting. You have a fascination with Africa?" He looked at me curiously as he pointed at the huge poster of the map of Africa.

"I don't know if I would call it a fascination, per se. I studied history in undergrad, with a minor focus on African history."

"You don't say." He looked impressed. "What do these colors on the map indicate?"

"Have you ever heard of the partition of Africa?"

"Can't say that I have." He shook his head.

"It was also known as the scramble for Africa."

"Like scrambled eggs?"

"Very funny." I rolled my eyes. "No, in 1884, there was a conference known as the Berlin Conference. The conference was held by Otto Von Bismarck. He was the first chancellor of Germany, if you didn't know."

"I can quite honestly say that I didn't know that."

"Well, essentially he and other European leaders met up and decided which countries in Africa each of them were going to get."

"Going to get?" He raised an eyebrow. "What do you mean?"

"I mean they were picking which countries they were going to colonize." I could hear myself getting heated. "Imperialism at its best."

"You sound like you're getting angry." He surveyed my face. "You okay?"

"I'm fine. I'm just passionate about history and how greed has affected so many people in the world. And yet, so many people have no idea."

"I get it." His lips thinned. "I learned things when I was in Afghanistan that I never would have guessed or known about."

"Yeah, I bet." I looked away then. "War zones aren't a great place to be."

"No, they're not." He reached forward and grabbed my hands. "Do you know anyone else who's been in the military?"

"Yeah." I looked away from him. "I do. Or I did."

"Oh?"

"He was stationed in Iraq for a couple of years and then in Afghanistan."

"Air Force?"

"No, Army." I started humming.

"The Army song?" He looked surprised. "You know it."

"First to fight for the right,
And to build the Nation's might,
And The Army Goes Rolling Along
Proud of all we have done,

Fighting till the battle's won,

And the Army Goes Rolling Along," I sang.

Max looked impressed. I felt slightly embarrassed to have gotten so caught up in the singing of the song.

"I don't know many civilians that know that song."

"My brother was Army," I said. "He taught it to me."

"Is he still in the army, then?"

"No." I didn't offer any other information. He seemed to understand that I didn't want to continue this line of conversation because he changed the subject.

"I deposited the first half of your money into your account this afternoon. I hope that helps," he said then walked back over to my bookshelf to look at the books.

"It does," I said. "Thank you."

"Why was it so important to you?"

"Not that it's any of your business, but I like to send care packages to the soldiers for Christmas." I looked down at my hands. "Nothing crazy, but the bare necessities and some little treats. I didn't think I'd have the money this year because *someone* got me fired."

"That someone being me?" He made a face. "I didn't know you sent care packages as well."

"What do you mean as well?" I said as I looked at his face. "As well as what?"

"I just meant I didn't know that you sent care packages to soldiers. That's nice." He turned away from me. "It means a lot to the guys. I know it meant a lot to me."

"I suppose your family must have sent you a lot of packages and stuff."

"Actually, no. They never sent me a package. Not once. I never received any letters either."

"Oh, wow." I felt sad for him. "Not once?"

"Not once." He turned around then and gave me a melancholy smile. "I suppose you can say that us billionaires don't have it all, after all."

"I never said you had it all." I tried to smile, but I felt sad for him. "I don't think money solves all problems, if that's what you mean. I don't have much money, but I don't think it's the be-all and end-all of the world."

"Even though it gets you vintage Chanel handbags?" he said, the corners of his eyes crinkling.

"I mean, vintage Chanel handbags are cute, and I love fashionable things, but I don't *need* them, need them." I walked over to him and touched the side of his face. "I don't really know you, and I know you have no reason to trust me, but I'm not all about money. I'm sorry. Sincerely sorry for using your name to benefit monetarily." I paused. "I truly didn't do it on purpose."

"I know." His face was expressionless as he stared at me. "How are you single?"

"What do you mean?" My eyes narrowed at him.

"You're a beautiful lady. A good person, from what I can tell. Why are you still single?"

"Why are *you* still single?"

"Deflecting the question, huh?"

"No." I shook my head. "I've experienced loss. Heartbreak. It's hard to bounce back from that."

"I understand." He stared into my eyes. "You still taking guitar lessons?"

"Guitar lessons?" I blinked at him in confusion. "What are you talking about?"

"Didn't you say that you used to play guitar?"

I froze for a few seconds, trying to remember if I'd mentioned that.

"No, I never said that." I shook my head. "I mean, I took a few classes in college. I wasn't good." I laughed then. "In fact, I was awful. The only people who know I took classes are Anabel and Emily. And the instructor."

And Brandon, of course. But I wasn't going to talk to him about Brandon.

My eyes narrowed at him. "How did you know?"

"Maybe it came up when I did my research on you?" He shrugged. "I had to learn more about you before I decided if I was going to sue you or see if we could come to some sort of arrangement."

"I suppose." I nodded. "I guess I did have that one video on YouTube of me trying to play 'Wonderwall' by Oasis." I cringed. "I knew I should have deleted that video."

"I'd love to see it."

"Oh hell, no." I laughed and shook my head. "I don't want anyone to watch that."

"I play the guitar." He smiled. "I could teach you some songs."

"Aww, I didn't know you played."

"Yeah, you're getting to know the real me." He grabbed my hand and pulled me towards him. "Not many people know the real Max Parker."

"Why's that?" I wrapped my arms around his neck. "I couldn't even find any photos of you online. Just one of you in college on the swim team or something."

"I don't like photos of me circulating." His expression grew shuttered. "The press knows not to publish any if they want to attend my press conferences, and I have friends at Google who've been good about deleting random pics that show up."

"But why do you care?"

"When you're rich, you become a target." He lightly kissed the tip of my nose. "It's easier for me to get around the city and the world without being accosted."

"I see." Though I didn't really. "You're not who I thought you were."

"And you're exactly who I thought you were."

"What does that mean?" I frowned.

"Nothing bad." He let out a deep sigh. "Life is funny, isn't it?"

"In what way?" I ran my hands down his chest before leaning my body into his. "Are you going to tell me what you mean?"

"I don't know if I should." His hands moved around my waist and ventured down to my ass. He squeezed my butt cheeks and moved me into him so that I could feel his hardness next to my stomach. "I want you so badly, Charlotte. I want to feel myself inside of you. I want to feel you on top of me. I want to feel your warm breath on my cock. I want to taste you. I want to lick up your juices. I want to hear you shouting out my name." He groaned loudly, his fingers creeping up the inside of my shirt and cupping my breasts again. "But we can't play these games."

"What games?" I whispered as I reached down and unbuckled his belt. It came apart easily now that I had better access. I undid his top button and reached my hands down his pants and into his boxer shorts. "I don't play games." My fingers found his cock and I squeezed gently as I ran my fingers down the length of his shaft. His whole body stiffened. "I want to taste you as well, Max. I want to make you come with my mouth and I want to hear you begging me to finish the job."

"Charlotte," He groaned, and I felt his body shudder slightly. "We can't do this."

"Why not?"

"Because this isn't the reason I reached out to you." He shook his head. "You want true love. You want a man that can give you everything you want."

"You don't know what I want." I moved my hand from out of his pants. "Maybe I just want to have some fun."

"Why did you agree to be my fiancée?" he asked me softly as he took a step away from me.

"Because I owed you."

"Is that the only reason?"

"What would be another reason?"

"I don't know. Nothing else, I guess." He shook his head. "I'm sorry I bought Sally's company and fired you. I didn't know you were that—" He stumbled over the words to say and I cut him off.

"Destitute?"

"Yes. Well, no, but you know." He made a face. "I do care about people."

"More than profits."

"Profits are important."

"Not more than people, though." I shook my head.

"Not more than you, no," he said softly.

I just stared at him, not knowing how to respond. What did he mean by that? He was confusing the hell out of me. The way he talked to me. The way he talked about me. The way he looked at me. Everything seemed so familiar. And yet, until a couple of days ago, I'd never met him before. Never even heard of him. Why did I feel so comfortable with him?

"What's that?" I asked as he moved suddenly and I saw a scar on the side of his abdomen that went all the way to his back. I reached out to touch it, but he pulled away from me.

"Just an old scar," he said and buttoned up his shirt. "Nothing much."

"Okay," I said, not wanting to push it further. He was clearly uncomfortable talking about it anymore. "Soooo, what's next? I'm fine with the contract as is. I'm ready to sign it."

"Good." He pulled out his phone. "Let's go back to my place, and then we can figure everything else out."

"Everything else like what?"

"Like if we're going to make this sexual or not," he said in a deadpan voice.

"You literally just told me you don't want to go there with me. Are you bipolar?" I stared at him. "You're going to give me whiplash."

"Sorry, this is confusing." He looked at his watch. "You've got 15 minutes to get ready. Then let's go back to my place, and we can chat over dinner."

"Okay," I said, not even bothering to argue at this point. I wanted to get to know him better as well, and if I was going to be his fake fiancée, then there was a lot I needed to know about him.

## CHAPTER 11

Charlotte: Guys, I cannot read Max at all. I don't know what to do.

Anabel: Didn't seem you were having much trouble reading him earlier.

Emily: Ooh, tell me more.

Anabel: I walked in on them having sex.

Charlotte: We were not having sex.

Anabel: His shirt was unbuttoned for another reason?

Emily: Dammmn, girl. You move fast.

Charlotte: We only kissed. A little bit.

Anabel: Where all did you guys kiss?

Emily: I need details.

Charlotte: Yes, my top is off. Nothing much happened. But I *did* feel something.

Anabel: And?

Emily: Do not leave me hanging here.

Charlotte: =====))))

Anabel: What the hell is that?

Charlotte: I'm guessing about eight inches. : P

Emily: Oh no way.

*Charlotte:* Way
*Anabel: I can't stop laughing.*
*Emily: Oh and BTW...*
*Charlotte: What?*
*Emily: 8=========D*
*Anabel: Hahahahahaha. Omg, I'm dying.*
*Charlotte: Trust you to school me on how to do a penis emoticon.*

I burst out laughing as I read Emily's text, and I could see Max staring at me from his seat in the car. I didn't look at him because I was trying to give him the silent treatment for a little bit. His hot and cold routine was getting on my last nerves, and frankly, I'd about had enough. I didn't know what was going on. Either he wanted me or not.

*Emily: So what advice do you need? Seems like you're doing fairly well already.*

*Charlotte: Okay, this guy is playing so hot and cold. I don't know if I'm coming or going. One moment, he's basically telling me to ride him and then in the next moment, he's acting like I'm his kid sister.*

*Emily: Hmmm. Weird.*

*Anabel: Have you asked him what's going on?*

*Charlotte: I don't really know what to say. I mean, I'm not about to say, look do you want to make me come or not?*

*Emily: I would ask that, :)*

*Anabel: No, you wouldn't*

*Emily: Yes, I would.*

*Charlotte: I'm with Anabel, Em. You would never ask a guy that.*

*Emily: Fine, just have some drinks tonight and maybe slip into his bed and see what happens.*

*Charlotte: That sounds so ... I don't know ... desperate.*

*Anabel: I'd just ask him, hey I'm finding it hard to read you, can you let me know what you want?*

*Charlotte: That sounds reasonable.*

*Emily: Boring! Take your panties off and put them in his pocket. Then whisper in his ear.*

*Charlotte: Whisper what?*

*Emily: Meet me at midnight in my bed if you want the ride of your life.*

*Anabel: You watch too much porn.*

*Emily: I'm just a good writer.*

*Charlotte: You two are cracking me up. I can't believe I'm doing this. This feels so Fifty Shades of Grey.*

*Anabel: Oh?*

*Charlotte: I'm in the back of a rich guy's limo wondering if he's going to try and make a move.*

*Emily: Did that happen in Fifty Shades? I can only remember the red room of pain or whatever it was called.*

*Anabel: Would you say yes if he invited you into his special room?*

*Charlotte: Hell no! I don't mind a little spanking, but I'm not interested in any flogging.*

*Emily: Would you use a strap-on?*

*Charlotte: A strap-on? You mean would I let him take me with a strap-on?*

*Emily: No, I mean would you wear one and pound him.*

*Charlotte: Eww, no!*

*Anabel: I told you. She's watching too much porn. Would you do that, Emily?*

*Emily: I don't know.*

*Anabel: You wouldn't do it.*

*Charlotte: There is no way you would do it.*

*Emily: I guess you guys know me better than I know myself. Maybe I've already done it.*

*Anabel: Girl, please. You told us that you were too scared to try anal. No way you'd be using a strap on.*

*Emily: I'm not \*scared\* scared. I just don't wanna shit. Shit during sex is not sexy.*

*Anabel: You don't always shit. And anal can feel good. In a different way.*

*Emily: Says the real porn Queen. : P*

*Charlotte: Guys, we are way off track here.*

*Anabel: Sorry.*

*Emily: Yeah, Anabel, get your mind out of the gutter. BTW, when are you going to Australia? I thought you were leaving tomorrow or something?*

*Charlotte: I'm not even sure what's going on, tbh.*

*Emily: I gotta admit, he does sound like he's all over the place. He's hot and he's rich, but he sounds like a hot mess.*

*Anabel: Maybe he's conflicted that he's taking advantage of the situation because he fired you.*

*Charlotte: Maybe. Oh shit, his hand is on my knee.*

*Emily: It's going down.*

*Charlotte: Nope, I just moved away. I'm ignoring him right now. I'm not going to play games.*

*Anabel: You go, girl.*

*Charlotte: Anyone free to go shopping tomorrow? He gave me the advance, and I want to put the packages together for the soldiers and get them sent out before it's too late.*

*Emily: I can help you.*

*Anabel: I would, but I have a long day tomorrow. Buy $100 worth of stuff for me. I'll Venmo you.*

*Charlotte: You don't have to do that.*

*Anabel: It's not for you. It's for Brandon.*

*Emily: <3*

*Charlotte: Love you, girls. We've just arrived. I'll text you both later.*

*Anabel: Have fun.*

*Emily: Do everything I wouldn't do.*

"Where are we?" I asked as I got out of the back of the limo. I was surprised that Max hadn't tried to get my attention when we were in the car. He'd touched my leg once or twice, but once he'd realized I was ignoring him, he'd stopped. I looked around the car garage. I'd thought we'd pull up outside a big building.

"We're at my home."

"Oh?" I stared at the cars next to the limo. "Here?"

"Obviously not in the garage." He chuckled. "Follow me, we'll take my private elevator up."

"Private elevator?"

"A perk of being rich."

"I suppose it is." I followed behind him through two stainless steel doors and then to a private elevator that was manned by a security officer.

"Good evening, Mr. Parker."

"Good evening, Vlad."

I looked at the security guard again. Was this the guy from the club? He was stocky and his face looked familiar, but I really couldn't tell. I didn't want to assume that security guards all looked the same, and the guy didn't look at me as if he'd seen me before. I was about to ask him a question when the elevator arrived and Max stood to the side to let me enter first. Once inside, he pressed the PH on the dashboard and then looked at me.

"Your bags will be brought up shortly. Are you hungry?"

"I'm not hungry." I shook my head. "I am a bit tired, though. Maybe I'll lie down."

"Okay." He nodded. "We can chat tomorrow." He paused. "I have company coming over this evening, so I'll be a bit busy. We can reconvene for our chat tomorrow."

"Uh huh." I pursed my lips. So Sandy was still coming over then, huh? I ignored the pangs of jealousy that hit me.

The elevator stopped, and I followed him into a huge penthouse that was full of wall-to-ceiling windows.

"Wow." I looked out over the New York skyline. "This is amazing."

"It's not bad," he said with a small smile. "Follow me."

I followed him down what seemed to be a never-ending corridor until we stopped at the last door. He opened it and I followed him in. He switched the light on and then swung his arm around the room.

"I think you'll find that this bed is a lot more comfortable than the couch you were sleeping on at home. In fact, I think it's most probably going to be one of the most comfortable beds you've ever slept on in your life."

"Wow, thanks." I stared at the king-sized bed with the clean white cotton sheets and could already imagine my weary body sinking into the mattress. "You didn't have to let me stay here. You know that, right?"

"I know that, but I wanted you to stay here." He looked at me for a couple of seconds with desire in his eyes and then he smiled slowly. "I thought it would be nice to have you close." He then proceeded to take two steps towards me. "I think I'll enjoy sleeping under the same roof as you."

"I guess it will be cool," I said with a small smile my heart racing as he took another step towards me. I was hoping he would pull me into his arms and ravish me, but he didn't do anything. "You didn't have to have me stay, you know. I really do love my apartment." I wasn't sure why I was going on about it, but I didn't know what else to say.

"I'm sure you really do love it, Charlotte. It's a pretty cute place. Small, but cute." He smiled. "Why didn't you get a one-bedroom?"

"I can't afford a one-bedroom." I laughed. " I was lucky to get a studio by the park in my price range."

"I guess you don't make much money."

"We're not all billionaires like you, Max Parker. We don't all own corporations." I walked over to the bed and sat down. It was as comfortable as it looked. "You know this is really comfortable." I lay back, my head hitting the pillow. Max stared down at me as I lay there, and I willed him to join me on the bed.

But he just nodded his head. "Relax," he said with a small smile. "I need to do some work. Let me know if you need anything."

"I thought you wanted us to talk tonight."

"No, another time." He cleared his throat. "I have some things to deal with tonight."

"With Sandy?" I sounded a bit bitter and tried to smile.

"You keep mentioning her name." He ran his hands through his hair. "Do you know her, by any chance?"

"Why would I know her?" I asked him. "I didn't research all your fuck buddies. I'm not a stalker."

"Okay." He nodded. "It's as I thought."

"What's as you thought?" I sighed. "You keep talking in riddles."

"It's been a long day. Just relax." And with that he was gone, closing the door behind him.

I sank down onto the bed and put a pillow over my head and screamed. I didn't want to be alone. I didn't want to stay here by myself. But I could feel my eyes closing. I really was tired. I said a monologue in my head that I remembered from school. It was the opening scene from Twelfth Night by William Shakespeare, and before I knew it, I was falling asleep and all my anger subsided.

※

THE PHONE RINGING NEXT TO MY BED WOKE ME UP, AND I picked it up after one ring. "Hello," I said, not even thinking.

"Oh, hi, can I speak to Max, please?" a soft, feminine voice asked. I looked at the alarm clock on my bedside table and saw that it was midnight.

I frowned. This really was a booty call.

"I'm afraid Max isn't available right now," I lied as I sat up in bed.

"Oh." She sounded hesitant and I wondered if she was curious who I was. "Is this Charlotte?"

I frowned. How did she know my name? Was she the woman he'd said he'd been dating? Had he told her about me?

"Yes, who is this?"

"This is Sandy."

"Okay, Sandy, do you have a message?"

"I just wanted to let him know I wasn't going to be able to make it over tonight after all."

"Okay, I'll let him know."

"Thank you." She paused. "I guess I'll see you soon."

"Yeah, bye."

I hung up. I didn't want to see her. I wanted Max to be done with her. Was the reason he wasn't sure about hooking up with me because he felt some sort of loyalty to Sandy?

I sighed and got up off the bed. I noticed that my two small cases were by the door and I started to pull off my dress so that I could change into pajamas. I pulled my bra off and unzipped my case. As I stood there in just my panties, an idea came to me. I grabbed a grey tank top and pulled it on. It didn't cover my panties, but that was the plan. I was going to pop to Max's bedroom to pass on the message from Sandy. I mean, I didn't want him to be up all night, possibly waiting for her arrival.

I grinned to myself as I headed out of the room and into the corridor. I paused for a few seconds as I realized I had no clue where Max's bedroom was. I moved to the right and then opened the next door I came across and peeked inside.

The room was dark, but I could see a treadmill in the corner illuminated by the streetlights, so I closed the door and made my way to the next one. I opened the door slowly and peered inside. Bingo! Max was in bed, lying flat on his back.

I walked inside slowly and made my way to his bed, being careful to not make any noise. I could see that he had a mask on his eyes, and I wondered if he would be able to tell that I wasn't Sandy. I crept onto his bed quickly and planted my lips on him. He reacted almost immediately kissing me back and running his hand down my back.

"I wondered if you were coming," he said in a husky voice and then he made to take his facemask off.

"No," I said softly, putting a hand up to stop him.

"Oh, you want to make it spicy?" He rolled over so that I was on my back and he was on top of me. I felt his fingers on my thighs, and he groaned as he ran his fingers across my skin. "You came prepared," he said, and I felt his fingers pulling my panties down and off of my legs.

His fingers then made their way between my legs and he rubbed my clit back and forth. I moaned at his touch and my body buckling slightly as he inserted a finger inside me. I reached up to bring him down to kiss me as he played with me. As his tongue darted into my mouth, I felt tingles of pleasure running all through my body. His fingers then ran up my stomach and pulled my top off. And I pulled him down into me so that I could feel his naked chest crushed against my breasts. I wrapped my legs around his waist and was disappointed to feel that he still had his briefs on. His hard cock rubbed me through the material, and I grabbed his ass so that I could feel him closer to me. He mumbled something incoherent against my lips, and I ran my hands through his hair, pulling on the short strands.

"I need to take this off." He reached up to take his mask off. "I need to see your face."

"It's not who you think it is," I said softly as he pulled it off. I waited to see the look of surprise on his face, but it never came. "It's me, Charlotte."

"I know." He grinned down at me. "I knew as soon as you walked into my room."

"How?" My jaw dropped.

"I would recognize your scent anywhere."

"Are you saying I smell?"

"Yes," he grinned. "In a good way."

"Is there a good way to smell?"

"Shh," he said and he placed a finger on my lips. "Too much talking, Charlotte."

"What do you want to do instead?" I said, feeling myself grow wetter as he looked into my eyes. How could this man be so damn sexy?

"This."

I felt his lips on my neck, then, kissing me softly, his tongue caressing my body as he made his way south. I gripped the sheets as his lips found my right nipple and I couldn't control my body's reaction as he sucked on my nipple and then started tracing his fingers down my thighs. His fingers ran up and down my thigh, inching closer and closer to my pussy, but he wouldn't touch it. I could tell he was teasing me, and it was driving me crazy. His lips left my nipples, and he kissed down to my stomach, licking my belly button before kissing further down. My body stilled as I waited to see what he was going to do next. I didn't have to wait long before I felt his tongue on my clit, licking me up and down and then sucking on it gently. I could feel my wetness covering his face and I felt myself coming as he stuck his tongue inside of me, moving it back and forth quickly. I gripped his shoulders as he pleasured me and my sobs of pleasure echoed around the room.

My body was shaking as he removed his tongue and

stood up to pull his briefs off. His cock sprang free and I gasped as I saw it in all of its glory. I hadn't been exaggerating when I'd said it was eight inches and I reached out to touch it. He stilled as my fingers played with him and I reached up and grabbed him and pulled him down onto the bed beside me. Before he could move, I started kissing down his body, loving the way he twitched as I got closer and closer to his cock.

"You don't have to." He gasped as I reached his cock and licked the length of his shaft. My fingers found his balls and I played with them gently. "Fuck." He groaned as I lowered my mouth and took as much of his cock into it as I could. "Oh fuck, Charlotte." His fingers reached down and pulled my hair as I opened my mouth wider and sucked him. I moved my tongue around his shaft as I sucked my lips together and slid his cock in and out of my mouth. He tasted salty and warm and extremely hard. I could feel myself growing wetter as I bounced up and down, and his groans were turning me on even more.

"Stop, I'm going to come," he said as he pulled me off of him. I looked down at his face to see him grinning at me. "The first time I come with you, I want to see your face."

I laughed as I slid on top of him. Moaning as I felt his hardness between my legs, I rubbed myself back and forth on him, grinding my clit into the tip of his cock, loving the feel of him beneath me. He reached up and played with my breasts as I continued to grind on him and I started to move a little bit faster. His hands then grabbed my hips, and I felt him reach down and position himself at my entrance. He moved the tip of his cock back and forth on my clit and I moaned at the feel of his fingers also rubbing next to me. He shifted at the same time I did and for one brief second the tip of his cock was inside of me and I sat up and bounced down on him, feeling the full length of him inside of me. He groaned and pulled out and rolled me over onto the side of the bed.

"Hold on." He reached over to the nightstand and grabbed something from a drawer. I watched as he ripped open the wrapper and pulled a condom onto his shaft. "Okay," he said and then he rolled over on top of me, positioning himself over me. I felt his lips on my neck and I arched my back so that my breasts were touching his skin. He moved a hand down to part my legs and then I felt his cock at my entrance again. He looked into my eyes then and he kissed me hard.

I felt him enter me, stretching me out as he thrust into me. I cried out as I felt the full length of him inside of me, but he didn't stop. He increased his pace and as he slammed into me, I felt his fingers once again playing with my clit, bringing me to a climax faster than I ever had before. My body quaked as he fucked me and he grinned as I reached up and scratched his back calling out his name in ecstasy.

"Don't stop!" I cried out as I felt my insides ready to burst with pleasure. "Oh Max, don't stop!" I screamed as my pussy tightened on his cock and I felt myself coming.

He increased his pace then and closed his eyes. His cock slammed into me and it felt like nothing I'd ever felt before in my life. He paused for a few seconds and then I felt his body shuddering as he came and collapsed on top of me.

He lay there for what must have been three or four minutes before he pulled out of me and took the condom off, dropping it on the bedside table. He scooped me into his arms and kissed my lips before pulling the sheets over us.

"I'd say that this was the perfect ending to the day with my new fiancée," he whispered into my ear, and as he played with my nipples, I silently agreed with him.

This wasn't how I'd pictured everything going down at all, but as I turned on my side and he held me from behind, I knew that I was happy with how it was going. I felt his cock growing against my ass, and I gasped as he slipped it in between my legs.

"You're hard again already?" I said as he bit into my shoulder. "Oh, Max."

"I'll let you sleep for a couple of hours before we go again." He laughed. "I'll let you savor round one before we move to round two."

I giggled and then found myself falling asleep, a satiated smile on my face.

## CHAPTER 12

The next morning, we had breakfast in his dining room, chowing down on cereal and pancakes. I'd been surprised when Max had made the coffee and pancakes himself. I would have bet he had a housekeeper or maid, but he said he only had a cleaner that came in every two weeks. After having been in the Army, he said he had no need of anyone to take care of him.

It had been fascinating watching him move around the kitchen. He knew where everything was, and the pancakes he'd whipped up had been absolutely delicious. I'd gone back to my room and showered, and as I'd put on a dress and some strappy heels, I remembered that I'd forgotten to tell him that Sandy had called the night before. I didn't really want to talk about her, but I knew it was rude to not give him the message. I left my room and hurried down the corridor to give him the message.

I could hear music playing in his room, and I paused to listen. It only took me a few seconds to realize that this was wasn't a stereo playing music. It was Max singing and playing his guitar. I opened the door slowly and walked in carefully so as not to disturb him. He was sitting on a gray couch on the far side of the room and his eyes were closed as he strummed. The song sounded familiar to me and my heart started thudding as I realized he was playing "Hallelujah."

He sounded just like Jeff Buckley as he sang and I couldn't believe how soulful his voice sounded. As I stared at him, I couldn't help but think of Brandon. Brandon and I had loved this song. We'd loved it almost more than life itself. This was Brandon's song.

*Don't go there, Charlotte.* A voice whispered in my head. *Stop. You cannot live in the past. No more.*

"Do you know any other songs?" I spoke up before I could stop myself. Max's eyes flew open and he looked up at me in surprise.

"I didn't hear you coming in." He stopped playing and put the guitar down. "What are you doing?" He looked me over and I walked over to him, loving the way his eyes took me in. "Nice dress. Pantyless?" He grinned as he tilted his head to the side as if it were an important internal debate he was trying to figure out the answer to.

"I have panties on. No easy access today." I did a little twirl before heading over to him. "I had a message for you. I wanted to give it to you last night, but uh, other things happened."

"Oh, what's the message?" He looked at me curiously.

"Sandy called that she wouldn't make it last night," I said and stopped right in front of him. "So I guess she's not over the rumors she heard about me." I stared at him poignantly, hoping he would give me more information about his relationship with her.

"What rumors did she hear about you?" His hands snaked around my waist. "What do you think you know?"

"I'm wondering if she was the woman you were sleeping with that heard the rumor that we were engaged?" My hands slid up his black t-shirt to touch his chest. His skin felt warm to the touch and I ran my fingers up to graze his nipples. He reacted swiftly by pulling me into him, and I gasped as I felt his fingers on my ass. Before I knew what was happening, he was picking me up and carrying me over to the bed and dropping me onto the mattress. He got onto the bed next to me and I felt his lips on mine.

"Or is she another woman?"

"She's another woman," he said as his hands slipped between my legs and moved up my thigh. His sharp intake of breath made me laugh as he groaned. "You lied. You're not wearing panties."

"Oops, I must have forgotten to put them on."

"You didn't forget." He chuckled as he touched me lightly. "Fuck, I'm so hard." He groaned and then kissed me hard for a few seconds. "But we don't have time right now."

"What?" I asked disappointed. "Why not?"

"We're going out."

"Where are we going?" I asked him, feeling frustrated as I sat up on the bed. I watched as he pulled his t-shirt off and pulled a crisp white shirt on. "Do you have to work?"

"Do I need to wear something a bit more professional?"

"No, you look fine. You look beautiful." He smiled. "I have a shareholders meeting today. I kind of can't miss it." He laughed. "As the CEO, they expect me to be there."

"Oh, haha, true." I blushed. "Do they expect me to be there as well?"

"No, but I want you there," he replied. "We'll have some fun." His eyes lit up as he surveyed me. "Maybe even a lot of fun."

"What does that mean?"

"I think you know."

"Max! It's your office, and it's a shareholders meeting. We can't get up to hanky panky."

"Hanky panky?" He laughed. "Is that what the kids are calling it these days?"

"Max."

"What? I own the company. We can do what we want." He licked his lips. "It will be fun."

"Is this part of my job description?" I stood up and walked over to him.

"Of course not." He cracked a smile. "Unless, of course, you think it should be."

"Well, if you're telling me that I'll get fired unless we embark on some crazy sex at your office, who am I to say no?" I grinned at him and he pulled me into him and kissed me.

"You're a naughty girl, Char bear," he said as he rubbed my back

I froze. Had he called me Char bear?

"Everything okay?" He looked at me with a worried expression. "You look like you've just seen a ghost."

"No, I'm okay. Your nickname threw me a bit." I ran my hands through my hair. "Someone I knew used to call me that." I immediately felt guilty for calling Brandon someone I knew. He was so much more than that. But if I mentioned his name, if I said who he was to me, then I'd have to say more and I couldn't. I didn't want to.

"Oh, sorry," Max said and he held me tight and kissed my forehead. He finally let me go and then he looked at his watch. "I need to shave real quick. Meet me by the front door in ten minutes?"

"Sure." I made my way to the door of his bedroom. "Oh and by the way, I think I will let you give me a guitar lesson at some point. I didn't realize you were so talented."

"I'm self-taught." He looked shy as he stared at me. "I learned when I was overseas."

"Oh?"

"On base."

"Oh."

"Yeah, I used to learn chords for songs the guys wanted to sing. My best friend encouraged me, actually." His eyes looked far away. "Whenever I ran out of ideas of songs to play, he would give me a long list of songs to learn."

"Oh, this was the friend who was like family to you?"

"Yeah, he was." He nodded. "He was the best friend I ever had. We used to call each other brothers."

"That's sweet. I'm glad you guys had each other." I nodded. "I know it's lonely out there. My ... well, someone I know, he loved getting letters from me." I looked away for a few seconds thinking. "I used to send him letters and care packages and cookies every couple of weeks." I bit down on my lower lip. "I didn't hear back from him that frequently, but I still sent them. I wanted him to know I was thinking of him."

"He must have been someone special to you." Max walked towards me. "Where is he now?"

"Back in Florida." My heart lurched as my words trembled. "Sorry, let me go and get ready. I'll meet you in the front in ten," I said and then I hurried towards the bedroom, tears threatening to fall. Why was it still so hard? Why did it still feel like yesterday? Memories came crashing down on me as I entered the bedroom.

*"I'll always be your first love, Charlotte." Brandon had said as he'd spun me around the room. "No guy will ever match up to me, and that's okay. Because I'll be here to take out anyone that ever hurts you." We'd both started laughing then because I'd stepped on his toes for the umpteenth time trying to learn how to waltz.*

*"No one waltzes at their high school prom, Brandon. I'll be fine." I'd said, and he'd just made a face.*

*Then there was the time he'd taken me to Disney World, and we'd been short $20 on the entrance fee to get both of us tickets. Who knew Disney cost so much money? We'd ended up going to SeaWorld instead* *and he'd bought me a stuffed dolphin to commemorate the day. I still had that dolphin in my parents' house. In my bedroom. It sat on the middle of my bed. Still. I knew they hadn't changed anything in my room. They hadn't changed anything in the house. Memories flooded the walls like rain that had never seeped away.*

*And then ... then there was the day he'd told me he'd enlisted. "They'll give me money for college, Char bear," he'd said. "I only have to go for four years. That's nothing." I hadn't liked it, of course. I hadn't wanted him to leave me. But I knew I was being unfair, but he hadn't consulted me at all. And that had hurt. "You're young, Charlotte, this isn't a decision for you to make."*

*I'd cried. I hadn't spoken to him for two weeks. It had been torture. I was being selfish. I had a scholarship to Columbia, and my parents were going to help me with any fees my loans wouldn't pay for. It had seemed like the best solution all around.*

*"I'll miss you so much."*

*I hadn't wanted to let go of him the morning he left for BCT. "Don't go!" I'd cried, but of course he'd had to go. He'd signed a contract. And he'd been excited. With his freshly cut buzzed crew cut. He'd looked older and more mature for some reason. And my heart had broken into a thousand pieces.*

*"I love you, Char bear." He'd blown me a kiss as he'd gotten into the car and driven away. It had felt like my life was ending in that moment. Only later did I find out how much worse that feeling could be.*

*And then he'd completed training and he'd come back home on a short visit. He'd looked thinner, more muscular, but happy. He'd been making friends. And he felt a camaraderie with his squad. He also really liked his sergeant, a man that been from Pensacola and also loved country music. I'd been happy for him, glad he was finding a purpose in his life that he hadn't before. I bought military history books and we discussed previous wars, we played Battleship, we lay under the stars and looked at the moon and talked. We did all those things you do with someone you love spending time with.*

J. S. COOPER

*And then came the call that he was going to be stationed in Afghanistan. He couldn't tell me exactly where. But there was an address I could write to that would make sure he got whatever packages and letters I sent. I didn't want him to go. I'd begged him not to go. Afghanistan. Just the name sent chills down my spine.*

*"It's not a tourist destination, that's for sure." He'd laughed and pulled me into a hug. "So don't worry. I don't expect you to visit." I hadn't laughed back. It wasn't funny. Him being in the army was so much more real to me now. I was proud of him—of course I was proud. He was a watchdog for my safety, for the entire country's safety. He was a fighter, a hero, a selfless gentleman in a sea of rogues. And I'd written him weekly. Sent him packages monthly. And I'd prayed for him every night.*

*Every single night.*

KNOCK KNOCK.

"Hey, Charlotte?" Max opened my bedroom door and walked in. "You okay? I've been waiting for you for the last fifteen minutes by the front door."

"Oh yeah, yeah, sorry." I rubbed my forehead. "I was thinking about something and got lost of time." I grabbed my handbag up and took a deep breath before turning to him. "Let's go."

※

*To: ArtyCharlotteJohnson@Gmail.com*
  *From: MaxParkerCEO@Parkercorporation.com*
  *Subject: When?*

DEAR CHARLOTTE,

*All I can think about is you riding me in front of this crowd of snoozers. You wouldn't believe how hard I am right now.*
*Max*


To: MaxParkerCEO@Parkercorporation.com
From: ArtyCharlotteJohnson@Gmail.com
Subject: Not right now


Dear Mr. Hard,
*There must be over two hundred people in this conference room. I won't be riding you anytime soon. Sorry.*
*Charlotte "Wet Panties" Johnson*


To: ArtyCharlotteJohnson@Gmail.com
From: MaxParkerCEO@Parkercorporation.com
Subject: Hard Cockadoodle doo


Dear Ms. Wet Panties,
*I know that is a lie as I know you have no panties on right now. I want to lick up your juices.*
*Max "Thirsty" Parker*


To: MaxParkerCEO@Parkercorporation.com
From: ArtyCharlotteJohnson@Gmail.com
Subject: Sorry not sorry


Dear Thirsty Boy,

*I'm afraid to say I put panties on in the bedroom. What do you think, I'm sort of boardroom whore?*
*Charlotte "Good girl" Johnson*


To: ARTYCHARLOTTEJOHNSON@GMAIL.COM
From: MaxParkerCEO@Parkercorporation.com
Subject: Liar


DEAR LEG TWITCHER,

*Do you need me to call a doctor? I can feel your legs twitching as I verify for myself that you have no panties on. Stop giving me dirty looks or the board and shareholders might wonder what's going on. Aren't you glad you wore a dress now? And that these tables off us so much privacy?*
*Max "Wet Fingers" Parker*


To: MAXPARKERCEO@PARKERCORPORATION.COM
From: ArtyCharlotteJohnson@Gmail.com
Subject: Stop


MAX!

*Stop it right now. If I throw my head back and start moaning, you will make both of us look like idiots.*
*Charlotte*


To: ARTYCHARLOTTEJOHNSON@GMAIL.COM
From: MaxParkerCEO@Parkercorporation.com
Subject: Come for me
*Dear Tight Pussy,*

*Come for me. I can feel that you want to. You're so bloody wet. I apologize in advance if I have to wipe my fingers on your dress.*

*Max "my zipper is undone" Parker*

To: MaxParkerCEO@Parkercorporation.com
From: ArtyCharlotteJohnson@Gmail.com
Subject: Hungry?

Dear Do you really expect me to cop a feel,

*I cannot believe you just sucked on your fingers. In a meeting. What are you thinking? And how could you exclaim, "yummy?" People are going to know what's going on!*

*Charlotte "Not grabbing your cock" Johnson*

To: ArtyCharlotteJohnson@Gmail.com
From: MaxParkerCEO@Parkercorporation.com
Subject: Lap

Dear Ms. Still Wet,

*I want you on my lap right now. Look down and you'll see my cock. Very hard. And very willing and ready. Sit that plump ass on my lap and ride me.*

*Max "About to bust a nut" Parker*

To: MaxParkerCEO@Parkercorporation.com
From: ArtyCharlotteJohnson@Gmail.com
Subject: Keep Dreaming

*You do know that that could be cause for arrest? Are you out of your mind? Put your cock back in your pants. Omg, are you jacking off? Max!!*

*To: ArtyCharlotteJohnson@Gmail.com*
   *From: MaxParkerCEO@Parkercorporation.com*
   *Subject: Touching not jacking*

*Dear Prim as a Rose Charlotte Johnson,*
   *A couple of strokes is not jacking off. You should know that. But thank you for helping out with the situation. I'm about to drop a pen. Get ready.*
   *Max "My tongue will make you come" Parker*

*To: MaxParkerCEO@Parkercorporation.com*
   *From: ArtyCharlotteJohnson@Gmail.com*
   *Subject: sgdggfgdfre*

*Max,*
   *Stop. jbasgufidfre. Huefcihuv. OMG!*

*To: ArtyCharlotteJohnson@Gmail.com*
   *From: MaxParkerCEO@Parkercorporation.com*
   *Subject: Quieter Please*

*Charlotte,*
   *I know I've made women lose their minds before. I didn't know I could make them lose their ability to spell. I'm going to guess that your*

*last email said. Max, omg, your tongue feels so good, omg, lick my clit harder, fuck me with your tongue, don't stop, don't stop, don't stop. :)*

*Good job on keeping quiet when you came, though you didn't have to squeeze your thighs quite so hard around my head.*

*Max "I can make women come under a table" Parker*


To: M‌AX‌P‌ARKER‌CEO@P‌ARKERCORPORATION‌.‌COM
From: ArtyCharlotteJohnson@Gmail.com
Subject: The woman on the right


M‌AX,

*The woman all the way on the right keeps giving me dirty looks. I think she knows what's going on.*

*Charlotte "I cannot look at anyone in the eye" Johnson*


To: A‌RTY‌C‌HARLOTTE‌J‌OHNSON@G‌MAIL‌.‌COM
From: MaxParkerCEO@Parkercorporation.com
Subject: Jealous


D‌EAR C‌HARLOTTE "‌TASTES LIKE HONEY‌" J‌OHNSON,

*She's just jealous. Why did you just drop a pen? You wouldn't?? Oh shit, but you would.*

*Max "nine-inch" Parker*


To: M‌AX‌P‌ARKER‌CEO@P‌ARKERCORPORATION‌.‌COM
From: ArtyCharlotteJohnson@Gmail.com
Subject: You don't taste like honey

*Dear Max "eight inches at most" Parker,*
*Did I hear you groaning just now when I had you in my mouth? You do know you were fucking my mouth and not my pussy, right? Though I suppose my head skills are just as good as sex. I didn't expect you to come quite so hard and fast though. Your cum is salty. Nothing like honey. And you got a bit on my dress. Hopefully, no one notices. When is the first break? I'm bored.*
*Charlotte "Deep Throat" Johnson*


*To: ArtyCharlotteJohnson@Gmail.com*
*From: MaxParkerCEO@Parkercorporation.com*
*Subject: Deep Throat*


*Dear Charlotte "You've had nine and a half inches in your mouth" Johnson,*
*We're in luck. The lights will be going out for a presentation in about fifteen minutes and we will be changing rooms. I say we're both in need of another release. You're going to need to sit on my lap, though. Play the doting fiancé and just pretend to be excited. I'll take care of the rest.*
*Max "I'm ready to come again" Parker*


*To: MaxParkerCEO@Parkercorporation.com*
*From: ArtyCharlotteJohnson@Gmail.com*
*Subject: Presentation*


*Dear Max Parker CEO,*
*Shouldn't you be paying attention to the presentation when it happens? Also, I can play the doting fiancé role well; I used to be an actress. Or rather, I always had dreams of being an actress.*

*Charlotte "I'm surprised your huge cock fits in my pussy" Johnson*

To: *ArtyCharlotteJohnson@Gmail.com*
From: *MaxParkerCEO@Parkercorporation.com*
Subject: *I'm surprised it fit in your mouth*

Dear Concerned fiancée,

*The presentation is something boring my execs put together to impress the board. I don't need to hear about my life again. I lived it. I know it. Also, I'm glad you recognize that my cock is huge. It's ready and waiting to come out to play again.*

*Max "Follow me out of this room" Parker*

To: *MaxParkerCEO@Parkercorporation.com*
From: *ArtyCharlotteJohnson@Gmail.com*
Subject: *This is so awkward*

Dear Mr. I have a movie made about my life,

*I feel so awkward sitting on your lap when everyone around is in their own seats.*

*Charlotte*

To: *ArtyCharlotteJohnson@Gmail.com*
From: *MaxParkerCEO@Parkercorporation.com*
Subject: *Your ass feels divine*

Dear Ms. "I'm about to fuck you hard" Johnson,

*We're sitting in the back seat. It's dark. Just enjoy what's about to happen.*

*Max*

*P.S. Try not to scream too loudly.*

I COULD FEEL MAX'S ARMS AROUND MY WAIST AS WE SAT AT the back of the large theater. He was cupping my breasts through my dress and moving me back on his lap so that I could feel his hardness underneath my ass. There were two men at the front of the room talking about Max and what a good CEO he was, but I found it hard to concentrate as I felt his hands slip under my skirt and move to the center of my thighs. His fingers traced lines along my skin and I could hear him breathing in my ear.

"I'm going to fuck you so hard," he whispered as he unzipped his pants and let his cock out. I could feel it between my legs now, hard and erect waiting to enter me, and I let out a light moan. His fingers started rubbing my clit and I closed my eyes and bit down on my lower lip to stop from crying out. He chuckled in my ear as he moved me back and forth on him and I wanted to beg him to enter him.

"I have to get my condom out first," he grunted, and I felt him searching in his pocket. He quickly ripped open the wrapper and his fingers brushed past my ass as he slipped the condom on. As soon as I knew he had it on, I stood up slightly, grabbed the head of his cock, repositioned it between my legs and sat back down, sliding down on his shaft. We both let out a slight moan as I took in all of his cock and started moving back and forth slowly.

"Fuck, you feel so good," he grunted. "Move a bit faster."

"It will be too obvious," I hissed as I moved gently back and forth. He increased his pressure on my clit and I felt his other hand on my hip, moving me faster. "Max!" I gasped as

## THE BILLIONAIRE'S FAKE FIANCEE

his cock filled me up and I slammed back down on him. I looked around to make sure that no one was watching us, but all eyes were ahead on the screen at the front. I looked up and saw a young Max playing with a toy train, and then a video of him swimming.

"This is a video of your life?" I asked in surprise, turning to look at him for a second. "You didn't say that."

"Hmmm." He just shrugged. "I don't know where they got those old videos from." He increased the pressure of his thumb on my clit. "Lean forward a bit," he said, and I obeyed his command. I'm not sure how he did it, but somehow this new position allowed him to thrust into me easier and he was now controlling the pace. I could feel my body tingling as he fucked me hard and I couldn't stop myself from swiveling my hips and bouncing back into him. "God, I could fuck you forever," he whispered as he held me to him. "I feel like your pussy was made for me."

"You're so romantic," I said with a small laugh as I felt myself about to climax.

"Come for me, Charlotte," he groaned as he slid in and out of me and rubbed my clit. "I'm not going to come until you do."

"I'm close," I gasped, and I was. I was on the brink of orgasm and I started to increase my pace to slam down just a little bit harder. "Ooh," I moaned, biting down on my hand. "Oh!" I cried out again as I felt myself orgasming on him. A few seconds later, I felt his cock shuddering inside of me.

"That was amazing," he murmured. He kept me on his lap, his cock still inside of me. I looked back up to the screen and watched as the video changed to one of him in the army. He was wearing his army uniform and I stilled at the image. That uniform. Oh, the memories. And then, like something out of a dream, the video changed and it was him in the barracks with some other men. And he had his guitar and they were singing. I smiled as I heard his voice, such a beautiful voice, but then the camera focused in on the other faces and I froze. I recognized someone else in the video.

"No," I whispered in shock. "No," I said again as the two men faced the camera.

"Hi, I'm Max and this is my best friend, Brandon," he said and they both waved at the camera. Max had known Brandon? He hadn't told me. *He hadn't told me!*

I jumped up off of his lap. "You lied to me."

He quickly zipped up his pants. "Charlotte, wait, please, I can explain."

"No, no, no!" I cried and ran out of the room through the side door. Thank God we'd been sitting at the back so nobody noticed me as I left.

"Charlotte, wait, please wait!" Max came running behind me, desperation in his voice as he caught up with me. "Charlotte, please, let me explain."

"What are you going to explain?" I shouted at him as I turned to look at him with tears streaming down my face. "Did you know?" I poked him in the chest. "Did you know?" I shouted louder this time. I could tell from the expression on his face that he knew. "So what was this?" I threw my hands up in the air. "What was all this? A sick joke?"

"No, it was never a joke. It wasn't meant to be like this. I just—I just wanted to meet you. To get to know you. I reached out to your parents to see if I could meet you, but they said it wasn't a good idea." He bit down on his lip. "You have to understand, this has been hard on me as well. I wanted to meet you. He talked about you so much. I felt like I knew you. He thought we would be friends, you know. He said that you'd hate me at first, but then—then you'd fall in love with me." His voice croaked. "I know this doesn't sound like enough. I know your heart is broken."

"Do you?" I shouted at him. "Do you really?" I stared at

## THE BILLIONAIRE'S FAKE FIANCEE

him, all the blood rushing from my face. "It was me that was home that day. Just me. And I opened the door and I knew. I saw their two faces, and I knew. Before they said anything."

"He didn't suffer." Max attempted to grab my hands. "The bomb, well, it killed everyone almost instantaneously." His face was white now as well. "I was in the infirmary. I should have been in the tanker too, but I'd gotten a case of pneumonia and it had lead to some bronchitis, so I was in bed." His voice choked. "I should have died as well. Some days, back then, I wished that I had."

"Don't say that." I shook my head. "No one should have died, you guys shouldn't even have been there."

"We were soldiers, Charlotte. That was our job." He shrugged. "We were needed there. We were protecting our country."

"And Brandon lost his life for it." Pain coursed through me. "He shouldn't have joined the army. He had his whole life ahead of him. It wasn't fair. It *isn't* fair."

"I know you loved him, Charlotte. He loved you. He talked about you all the time. He read all of your letters aloud. I got to looking forward to them almost as much as he did. And when you sent photos, I thought you were the most beautiful woman I'd ever seen. So stunning and sweet and funny. You made us laugh on days when there was nothing to be happy about. You brought joy and hope to our lives." He gave a wry smile. "I know that you thought you were only writing to Brandon, but what you wrote, it gave me reason to be happy as well."

"You guys must have been close."

His blue eyes looking strained and devastated. He didn't look so powerful and undefeatable anymore. "He was my best friend. The very first person in my life that was really and true a friend and a brother to me. He was going to come to

New York when he got out." He looked away then. "He was going to work with me."

"I didn't know that."

"There are other things you didn't know." He took a deep breath. "I wanted to meet you. When he died, I knew you'd be devastated. I wanted to tell you that he lived a good life at the end. He was happy."

"You didn't come to the funeral." My eyes narrowed. "If you were his best friend, why didn't you come? And why did you hide this from me?" I thought for a moment. "You knew before we ever officially met who I was, didn't you?"

"Yes."

"Did you know you were buying my company?"

"Yes." He sighed. "But that didn't go how it was supposed to. My HR office was meant to call you in about getting you into a different role in the corporation. You weren't meant to be fired."

"Oh?" I was surprised. "I didn't know that. That didn't happen."

"I know." He looked mad. "And trust me, I was going to get to the root of the issue, but then I heard you were going around the city saying you were my girlfriend, and I thought to myself, well isn't life strange? You can't make this shit up."

"How did you find out?"

"The boutique you got the handbag from, well, I used to date the owner. She called me." He shrugged. "I figured I could have HR call you, or I could see what happened next."

"So you decided to see what happened next?"

"Yes." He ran his hands through his hair. "I'm not proud of myself, and if I were to do it again, maybe I'd do it all a little differently. I wanted to come to the funeral, I did. But I was hurting too. I got hurt in Afghanistan, nothing major, but I was in the hospital."

"Your scar?" I asked him with a slight shiver, and he nodded.

"I wanted to pay my respects, and I wanted to meet you, but I couldn't go to the funeral. I called your parents, explained who I was, and asked to meet you and them, but they said you'd taken it hard. They said that they didn't think it was a good idea for you to meet any of his army friends." He paused. "I tried to understand, I tried to stay away. I wanted to respect their wishes, but I knew Brandon would have wanted us to meet. And I knew the girl that had written those letters would be someone I'd want to know. Maybe it was selfish of me. Maybe I should have just stayed away. I didn't mean to hurt you, Charlotte. I never wanted to hurt you. I just wanted to meet you. And once I did, I fell in love with your spunk and your spirit. I love the way you're witty and funny and crazy and over the top, and yet you're so sweet and loving. I don't want you to think I'm crazy or obsessed. I know you don't know me that well, but I've known you in my mind for years. And you're even better in person." He stopped then and half laughed. "I'm sounding like a crazy man, aren't I?"

"No." I finally reached over to take one of his hands in mine. "I think I understand." I took a deep breath. "My parents haven't gotten over Brandon's death, and maybe that's why it's been so hard for me to emotionally deal with it as well. You see, they had him five years before they had me. He was their firstborn, their perfect little blond-haired boy and he was the most loving, sweetest ..." My voice caught as I thought of Brandon. "He was the best brother a girl could ever have. He did everything for me that he could. He took me out to the movies. He took me shopping. He taught me how to surf. He helped me study. And he loved me so hard. He made me believe that I was special and beautiful and that any man would be lucky to have me." Tears fell down my face as I spoke. "I loved him so much, Max." I could hardly talk properly as I sobbed. "I loved him more than life itself. He was the best big brother. We were meant to grow old together. We were meant to play with each other's kids. We were meant to take joint family holidays together."

Max pulled me into his arms, and I rested my head on his shoulder and sobbed into his suit jacket, not caring that my mascara was most probably running.

"It's okay, Charlotte." He stroked the back of my hair. "It's okay," he whispered as he comforted me. "It'll be okay. I really, really hope you can forgive me." He sounded so stressed out that I finally looked up and into his eyes.

"I think I can forgive you, Max," I said with a sweet smile. "Is it true that you love me?"

"How could I not love you?" He grinned as he gave me a quick kiss on the lips. "You're my fiancée, right?"

"I'm your fake fiancée," I laughed. "And only because I was your fake girlfriend first."

"I never in a million years would have guessed you would have done that." And then he chuckled slightly. "Actually, that's not true."

"What do you mean, that's not true?"

"Do you remember the letter you sent Brandon where you told him you pretended to love heavy metal so that you could impress some guy you met in an English lit class?" He grinned at me, and I groaned. "I'm thinking the girl who can pretend to be into Black Sabbath could pretend that a hottie like me is her boyfriend."

"You're so full of yourself, Max." I wiped away some of my tears. "Who said you're a hottie?"

"You don't think I'm a hottie?"

"You're okay."

"Just okay?"

"Maybe a little bit more than just okay."

"Okay enough to become your real boyfriend?"

"You want to be my boyfriend?"

"I want to be your fiancé." He looked at me with loving eyes. "Your real fiancé, but it's a bit soon for that. I want to woo you first and then give you the proposal you've always dreamed of."

"How do you know I've dreamed of a proposal?" I asked and then groaned. "Oh, Brandon. He didn't keep many secrets, did he?"

"I'm glad he didn't." Max smiled at me. "You haven't answered my question yet."

"Your question?" I pretended to be confused and he groaned.

"Charlotte Johnson, will you be my girlfriend?"

"I have two questions first." I took a quick step away from him.

"Ugh, sure, what?" He folded his arms and waited for me to continue speaking. "You're killing me here."

"Why were you so hot and cold with me about sex and stuff?" I asked him, blushing slightly as I spoke.

"Hot and cold?" He looked confused and then smiled. "Oh, I was very much hot, but I didn't want you to think I was abusing my power or taking advantage of you. I wanted you from the moment I laid eyes on you." He grinned. "Hence that kiss by your elevator that night, but I wanted to respect Brandon and the fact that you were his sister and try and wait a little bit. But you're a little tease and sexy as hell, and I just couldn't resist any longer."

"Haha, okay," I said, pleased with his answer. "One last question, who is Sandy?"

"Oh ... Sandy?" He looked slightly guilty for a few seconds and then laughed. "This is my fault. You assumed something, and I didn't correct your mistake."

"What did I assume?"

"You assumed that Sandy was my lover," he said with a wry grin. "I'll admit I liked seeing you jealous, but that was never my intention. Sandy was in the army with me and Brandon. In fact, you could kinda say that she and Brandon were dating. A little bit. Not that we would ever have been able to admit it on base."

"Sandy was Brandon's girlfriend?" I blinked in confusion. "But you called her from your office. You told her to come over that night."

"She wanted to meet you," he said softly. "She wasn't coming to hook up with me. Charlotte, we were in the office making out. I wouldn't call another woman. What do you think I am?"

"I don't know," I said, but all of a sudden I felt lighter. "So Sandy isn't your booty call?"

"No."

"What about the girl that got upset because she heard about my lies?"

"She didn't exist. I just made her up to make you feel bad."

"What about the articles?"

"I leaked the news to the press." He gave me a wicked look. "I know, I know, I'm horrible. I just wanted to ensure that I could have you in my presence daily. Once I met you, I couldn't stop thinking about you. Obviously, in retrospect, I realize that I could have done things a little differently."

"I guess I could have as well." I laughed and leaned forward to kiss him again. "And the answer is yes, Max. I'll be your girlfriend. In fact, I'd absolutely love it."

His eyes lit up at my words then and he pulled me closer to him. I felt his hands on my ass and I wrapped my arms around his waist as well. "I think I'm falling for you as well, Max Parker," I said softly as he kissed me hard. "In fact, I think I already have."

# EPILOGUE

# T wo Months Later

*To: ArtyCharlotteJohnson@Gmail.com*
  *From: MaxParkerCEO@Parkercorporation.com*
  *Subject: Your Friends*

*Dear Charlotte,*
  *You know I love your friends, but why is it that Emily seems to spend more time at our house than I do? I'm in the office typing this email, but I'd much rather be in the living room, eating your pussy.*
  *Max "I'm too patient" Parker*

*To: MaxParkerCEO@Parkercorporation.com*
  *From: ArtyCharlotteJohnson@Gmail.com*
  *Subject: No one has ever called you patient*

*Max,*

*Emily is one of my best friends, and when I moved in here last month you did say that this was now my home as well. And Emily knows that my home is also her home. So you can expect to see her here a lot. Unless she gets a boyfriend. Do you have any single friends for her?*

*Charlotte "Guess what I got today" Johnson*


To: *ArtyCharlotteJohnson@Gmail.com*
From: *MaxParkerCEO@Parkercorporation.com*
Subject: *Inside*


*Dear Charlotte,*

*Are you finally on the pill? Do I get to feel all ten inches inside of you? Fuck. I'm hard just thinking about it. Get her out of our house in the next ten minutes and I'll have a long list of guys for her to date.*

*Max "I'm about to make you come" Parker*


To: *MaxParkerCEO@Parkercorporation.com*
From: *ArtyCharlotteJohnson@Gmail.com*
Subject: *Are they good guys?*


*Max,*

*I don't want you to set Emily up with random men. I need you to curate a list of thoughtful, good looking, honest guys. And yes, I'm on the pill. Though that doesn't mean we can't still use a condom. The pill isn't 100% safe.*

*Charlotte "I have no panties on" Johnson*

*To: ArtyCharlotteJohnson@Gmail.com*
*From: MaxParkerCEO@Parkercorporation.com*
*Subject: I will fuck you in front of your friend*


*Charlotte,*

*I love you. And I love your friend. And I will find a good guy for her to date. But if she's not out of this house in five minutes, she will find herself in the middle of a live sex show. And I don't know if you want her to know what your O face looks like.*

*Max "I need to come soon" Parker*


*To: MaxParkerCEO@Parkercorporation.com*
*From: ArtyCharlotteJohnson@Gmail.com*
*Subject: Love*


*Max,*

*I love you too. And I would hate for us to have our first real argument because you showed my friend your dick. I don't want her to laugh in your face. She watches a lot of porn. She won't be impressed.*

*Char*


*To: ArtyCharlotteJohnson@Gmail.com*
*From: MaxParkerCEO@Parkercorporation.com*
*Subject: My hand*


*My hand is going to be slapping that ass of yours in less*

*than five minutes. And then I'm going to make you come while you're on your knees looking out at the New York skyline. With my very impressive cock.*

To: *MaxParkerCEO@Parkercorporation.com*
From: *ArtyCharlotteJohnson@Gmail.com*
Subject: *Impressive is a subjective word*

*Some might say impressive. Some might say average. My ass is waiting for your hand. My pussy is waiting for your tongue. And my lips are waiting for your cock.*

To: *ArtyCharlotteJohnson@Gmail.com*
From: *MaxParkerCEO@Parkercorporation.com*
Subject: *Fuuck*

*You love being a dirty girl, don't you?*

To: *MaxParkerCEO@Parkercorporation.com*
From: *ArtyCharlotteJohnson@Gmail.com*
Subject: *What are you waiting for?*

*Emily left three minutes ago. I'm on the couch, naked, and if you don't come to take care of me soon, I think I'll have to use my new vibrator.*

To: *ArtyCharlotteJohnson@Gmail.com*

*From: [MaxParkerCEO@Parkercorporation.com](MaxParkerCEO@Parkercorporation.com)*
*Subject: Trash*

*I THREW ALL YOUR VIBRATORS IN THE TRASH. YOU DON'T NEED them anymore. I'll be there in five seconds.*

MAX CAME RUNNING DOWN THE HALLWAY, TUGGING HIS clothes off, and I laughed as I lay there looking up at him. My finger was on my clit, and he growled as he saw me pleasuring myself. I leaned my head back and smiled at the possessive look on his face as he dropped to his knees in front of the couch.

"This pussy is all mine," he growled as he grabbed my fingers and put them in his mouth and sucked. His blue eyes sparkled as he took in my naked body, then he buried his face between my legs and started sucking on my clit. I closed my eyes and grabbed his hair as he pleasured me with his tongue and I let out an audible sigh as he pulled his tongue out of me and pulled me to the ground and placed me on all fours. He came up behind me and then positioned his cock against my clit and rubbed gently.

"Fuck, you're so wet. You want this so badly, don't you?"

"Maybe," I gasped as he slid inside of me, and I leaned forward slightly as I lost my balance. He grabbed my hips and thrust into me hard and I could feel my ass bouncing back against his stomach. He slid into me deeper and harder, grunting.

"Oh shit," he groaned as he pounded into me a few more times and then exploded inside of me. "Sorry," he said as he pulled out of me and lay me down on the rug. "That just felt so good. I wasn't able to stop myself."

"That's okay," I moaned as his fingers slipped between my legs and rubbed me. "This feels good as well."

"I love you so much, Charlotte." He kissed my neck. "Are you happy here with me?"

"I'm happier than I've ever been in my life." I gasped as he slipped two fingers inside of me. "And I love you too, Max. Oh fuck, I love you!" I cried out as he kissed down my body and then entered me with his tongue. It didn't take me long to climax, and when I did, I looked up to see him staring down at me with happy eyes.

"Your parents are arriving tomorrow," he said as he played with my breasts. "I think we need to get prepared for their visit."

"Oh, how so?"

"We need to fuck in every public space possible the rest of the night." He grinned as his fingers gingerly touched my lips. "Because once they're here, we'll only be able to fuck in our bed and bathroom."

"Max." I giggled as I touched the side of his face. "You're such a bad boy."

"And you wouldn't have me any other way, would you?" He ran his fingers down my cheek and paused for a few seconds before he spoke again. "Growing up, I never really knew what it was to know love. Or to be loved. I didn't want for much, but I had no real purpose in life. But then I joined the army and I met Brandon, and I knew what it was like to be loved by a friend. And to love a friend. And he loved you. And he talked about you. And he read your letters, and a part of me fell in love with you. But then I met you. And you were so much more than Brandon had said, so much more than the letters, so much more than the photos. You were this beautiful, sexy woman that I couldn't get enough of. And as I've gotten to know you better, I've fallen harder and harder. I love you so much that I don't even know if it is possible for anyone to love someone as much as I love you. I think about you every second of the day. And I dream about you at night. You are always with me. You are the air that I breathe, Charlotte. I love that you love me, I love that you love your friends. I love every little perfect and imperfect thing about you. I want to spend the rest of my life loving you, Char Bear. And fucking you." He laughed. "That part's important as well."

"I love you too, Max. You're so much more than a billionaire. So much more than a hottie. So much more than a man that wishes he had a ten-inch penis." I giggled as he pulled me over his lap and gave me a small slap on the ass. "Oh Max, that doesn't even hurt."

"It's not meant to hurt, my love," he said softly, but he smacked me a little harder this time. I wiggled in his lap as he smacked me again and then slid a finger between my legs and rubbed. "I would never hurt you intentionally. I'm all about the pleasure," he growled and then he turned me over and lay back. "Ride me," he ordered with desire in my eyes.

"You're hard again? Already?"

And instead of answering me with words, he shifted my body so that I was sitting on his hardness and that was my answer. I smiled down at him and reached down to kiss him on the lips before sliding down onto his shaft.

"Show me what you got, big boy," I whispered against his lips, and he proceeded to do just that.

THE END

THANK YOU FOR READING, AND I HOPE YOU WILL LEAVE A review of the book. I sincerely hope you enjoyed Max and Charlotte's story as much as I loved writing this book. There will also be a book for Emily called About Last Night and a book for Anabel called When We Were Us. Both are available for preorder now. Continue reading for an excerpt from *About Last Night*. Please join my mailing list here so you don't miss either of the releases.

# EXCERPT FROM ABOUT LAST NIGHT

About Last Night

*Emily Johnson, twenty-five, college graduate, hot mess, lover of all things cheese. Hasn't had a date in a year.* Yeah, that's not something I would put in a dating profile. Ever. In fact, I can't be bothered to date. There are so many awful guys out there. I much prefer to Netflix and chill with a pizza. But of course, my busybody best friend Charlotte was having none of that. So she set me up on a blind date. Which I went on very reluctantly.

*Liam Montgomery, forty, rich, cocky, wears a Rolex, likes expensive whiskey, completely out of my league.* He was not who I would have chosen to have gone on a blind date with. Just because he was gorgeous didn't mean he would make a good boyfriend. Plus he was way too old for me. That didn't stop me from flirting with him, though. Or from spending the night with him. One long, very exciting night. That I'm never telling a soul about. Ironically, it turned out that Liam hadn't even been my intended date.

Unfortunately for me, hot-mess Emily, the biggest shock of my life was still to come. For while Liam and I should never have been, he's not about to leave my life quite that easily. You see I'm spending the holidays with my folks and Liam is also there. Only this time, he's not alone.

## CHAPTER 13

"Emily, you deserve to have find a good man." My best friend, Charlotte, gave me a pep talk on the phone as I ran along the street like a mad woman. "Just enjoy the date and have a good time." Her voice was light and happy, and I tried not to roll my eyes at her words. Just a few months ago, she'd been down on men as well, but now that she'd found love, she felt everyone should be searching for it.

"You know I hate blind dates," I rasped as I glared at the traffic light, willing it to change to green so that I could cross the road. "This is not what I want to be spending my Friday night doing." I was breathing hard from running and I was ready to curse someone out. How was I this out of shape? Didn't I go to the gym two times a week to ensure I didn't run out of breath when I ran? *No, you go to ogle the hot guys*, a little voice whispered inside of my head.

"You'd rather be watching Netflix and eating pizza?" Charlotte said in her judgmental voice. Once again, I tried not to roll my eyes. Who was she to judge me? At least Netflix didn't break my heart, and pizza only added to my weight, not my stress levels.

"Uhm, just three months ago, we were watching Netflix together," I reminded her as I slowed down. My calves were burning from the running and I was wishing that I had gone to those Zumba classes I'd signed up for. Obviously, walking on the treadmill staring at hotties pumping weights had done nothing for me.

"Yes, but now I have Max, and I want you to find love like I have." Charlotte was almost singing, and I wanted to gag.

"Charlotte, you've been dating Max for three months." I crossed the street. "How can you be in love already?" I didn't add, *How can you love a guy you started off hating?* because I knew she wouldn't wanna hear it.

"Emily, once the love bug hits you in the face, you know it. It doesn't matter if it's three days or three months." Charlotte laughed. "Now don't forget to give this guy a chance."

"What's his name again? Peter Jackson?" I look up and down the street, trying to locate the small wine bar where I was meeting my date. I couldn't believe that I'd agreed to this, but Charlotte and our other best friend, Anabel, had convinced me to give it a shot. I'd agreed, not because I was looking for love but because I knew this wine bar was meant to be one of the best new venues of 2020. And who was I to say no to a free drink?

"*Piers* Jackson," Charlotte corrected me. "He's one of Max's business partners."

"Okay," I stop outside the bar to reapply my lipstick and pat my hair down before entering the bar. "Ugh, I'm so not ready for a date."

"Relax, Emily, you're going to have a good time. Trust me."

"I just don't think this is a good idea, plus Jack called me this morning. He wants us to meet up."

I waited for Charlotte to answer, but silence followed after my words. She hated my ex-boyfriend Jack, and she had reason to. He'd treated me horribly and ended our relationship so that he could date other women. He'd broken my heart, and I had no idea why he now wanted to meet up with me again. But of course I'd said yes. I wanted him to beg me to get back with him, just so I could say no.

"I hope you told him to go to hell."

"You know I can't do that." I bit down on my lower lip.

"Why not?"

"Because he's my first love."

"Girl, that guy is a douche bag."

"Look, I'm here. I have to go."

"Have a great time, and tell me all about it when you're done."

"Won't you and Max be too busy making love to talk to me?"

"Haha, Emily." Charlotte laughed. "Max's working late tonight, so he's not coming by until tomorrow morning."

"Well, okay, then. I'll call you later." I hung up, took a few breaths, and walked into the bar. This was the first date I had been on in two years, and to say I was nervous was an understatement. I hadn't wanted to go on this date, but when Charlotte had set it up behind my back, I'd gone along with it, even though I was pretty sure the guy was not going to be a winner. Charlotte hadn't shown me a photo of him and had kept reminding me to be "open-minded." I had a pretty strong feeling that meant my date was going to be ugly, but at least I'd get a free meal out of it and some drinks. And by the looks of this place, they weren't going to be cheap. I walked up to the hostess and smiled.

"Do you have a reservation?"

I nodded, trying to remember my dates name. Shit! I'd already forgotten.

"Peter?"

She shook her head. "No one by that name here." She

gave me a snooty look, and I refrained from making a catty remark about her cheap looking blonde extensions. *Keep it classy, Emily!*

"Okay ..." I looked around the bar, and I saw a man sitting at a table at the back in a dark suit looking around the restaurant. When he saw me, he gave me a little wave.

"I think I see him." I guess Charlotte had shown him my photo. How unfair that he could know what I looked like, but I couldn't know what he looked like.

"Would you like me to walk you back?" the hostess asked.

I shook my head and brushed past her, trying to get a better look at my date. Right off the bat, I noticed that the man was gorgeous. He had a full head of dark hair and sparkling blue eyes, his suit was dark and he had a serious expression on his face.

"Hi, sorry I'm late." I slid into a seat across from him at the table.

"Sorry, what?"

I studied him unabashedly, taking in his stubble and jawline, then I leaned back and just started laughing.

"Something funny?" he asked.

"It's just that I know Charlotte told me to be 'open-minded,' but boy, how old are you?" I said, forgetting my manners. "Sorry, I'm not trying to be rude, but you're at least, what? Twenty years older than me?" I went to reach for my phone to text Charlotte, but stopped myself. "Don't get me wrong, you're handsome and obviously successful, but I just don't date older guys."

"Date?" The right side of his lip twitched slightly as he looked me over once again. "You think I want to date you?"

"Well, I'm not saying that you want to marry me, but you obviously agreed to this blind date based upon what I look like, and now I know why Charlotte didn't want to show me your photo."

"Why's that?"

"Because you're just a bit old for me." I looked into his amused blue eyes. "Not that you're not handsome and all, but like I said, I'm just not that into older men."

"How old are you?"

"Twenty-five," I replied and then because I couldn't stop myself, "How old are you?"

"Forty," he said smoothly. "So, not quite twenty years older than you."

"Yeah, I guess only fifteen."

"Still too many years on you?"

"Yeah." I nibbled on my lower lip. "Not to be rude or anything, but I prefer to date guys under thirty."

"Understandable." He nodded and sat back. "So, I suppose this blind date is over before it has even started?" He picked up a small glass of what looked like whiskey and took a sip. "A pity."

He leaned back, and all of a sudden, I could feel my body warming at his once over. He was older, but he was the hottest man I'd ever seen in my life. And if he kept looking at me in the way he was looking, then I didn't know what would happen.

"Well, I mean, we could always have a drink and eat or whatever. I did come all the way here," I said, taken aback by the fact that he didn't seem annoyed at my comments and hadn't asked me to stay. Did he not like me?

"I do not want to make you stay here against your will." He smirked. "I'm sure you have many other dates to go on. Other men to meet and enjoy your Friday night with."

"Well, you know." I looked away now, a bit embarrassed. Something in his supercilious tone suggested that he knew that I didn't go on many dates. "I have options," I lied, and he chuckled.

"Of course, a young girl like you would." There was a

touch of sarcasm in his voice. I looked into his eyes again and studied his face. He was really quite handsome. Uncomfortably, I realized that he was probably out of my league. "I don't want to keep you if you want to leave. A blind date with an old scrooge like me was obviously not in your plans tonight."

"Well, I mean, I can stay for one drink," I said, and my eyes dropped to his hands. His fingers were long, tan, and perfectly manicured. He wore an expensive-looking watch on his wrist. I was actually quite surprised that he agreed to a date with me. "So what's your deal, you seem like a cute guy, why are you here?"

"Why am *I* here?" He looked taken aback at my comment.

I was about to say something him when the waiter approached the table. He looked at me in confusion and then back over at my date.

"It's okay," my date said with a small nod. "Would you like something to drink ..." His voice trails off. "Sorry, remind me of your name?"

"You don't even remember my name?" I give him a look and shake my head. "Wow, did you just come to get laid?"

"Do you remember my name?"

"Yes, Mr. Peters. I mean, Jackson." I blushed at my mistake, and I could see he was amused.

"And my first name?"

"Do you remember mine?" I said, feeling embarrassed at pushing it again. "I'll have a glass of pinot noir, please." I gave the waiter a big smile.

"So you're still willing to drink with me? Even though I'm old?"

"It's been a long week." I sat back and sighed. "I hope you don't think I'm rude."

"Not at all." He sat back as well and studied my face. "So, tell me why this week has been so long?"

"So, how much did Charlotte tell you?"

"Charlotte?"

"Max's girlfriend." I paused and squinted at him. "You've met her, right?"

"No, I can honestly say that I haven't."

"Ugh," I groaned. "I'm going to kill her. She made it seem like she set it up after she met you. I guess she must have begged Max to find me a date, like I'm some sort of loser."

"You don't strike me as a loser."

"Thanks." I grinned at him. "I'm going to tell you something. You're kinda cute, you know that."

"Thank you." He smiled at me. "You're kinda cute, too."

"Just cute?"

When he grinned at me in response, my heart fluttered slightly. I stared at the top of his crisp white shirt and wondered what he would do if I started to undo his red tie.

"Are you fishing for a compliment?" He grinned as he took another sip of his whiskey. "Surely you wouldn't be flirting with an old man."

"I never said you were an old man," I said, my face burning. "I just said you were older than anyone I would ever choose to go on a date with. You know." I bit down on my lower lip, knowing that I hadn't made the situation any better. "I mean you're cute and all, but I'm just not ..." My voice trailed off as his grin grew wider and wider. I was making a real fool of myself.

"So, do you want to tell me why you chose to go on a blind date when you so obviously didn't want to?"

"It's not that I didn't want to." I hesitated, not wanting to offend him any more than I already had. "It's just that it's hard to make a right match." I'm trying to be polite now, seeing as he will hopefully be buying my wine and maybe a juicy steak dinner as well.

"I'm guessing you've had some bad dating experiences."

He took another sip from his glass and he smirked. "Obviously, you're dating younger men?"

"Well, maybe." I stared at his long smooth fingers. He had perfectly trimmed nails. I could tell that he was a man that took care of himself.

"Have you ever had an orgasm?"

My eyes flew back up to his face. "Sorry, *what*?"

He grinned. "I figured I could ask you anything, seeing as you've already dismissed me as a potential date? Am I right?" He put his glass down and leaned forward on the table, his blue eyes sparkling.

"Well, uh ..." My skin felt hot, and my eyes were glued to his pink lips as he licked them slowly. I couldn't avert my eyes from my movement and I wondered what his lips would feel like on my skin.

"Are you blushing or are my eyes deceiving me?" He laughed and threw his head back. "You don't have much experience with men, do you?"

"I have plenty of experience." All of a sudden the air between us had changed, and I could feel my heart racing. I'd never been on a date with this much sexual tension before. It was kinda exciting.

"If you thought I was too old when you saw me, why did you sit down and stay?" His blue eyes pierced into mine, and I swallowed hard.

"Because I wanted a free bottle of wine," I admitted, and he burst out laughing.

"You're very honest, aren't you?"

"Something like that." I nodded and then because I couldn't help myself I continued. "Why are you still entertaining me? I've been so rude to you. Why didn't you just get up and leave?"

"Maybe because I came here to enjoy a meal." He raised an eyebrow at me. "Shouldn't it be *you* who left?"

"Why didn't you ask me to leave, then?"

"Because I find you amusing."

"Oh?" I wasn't sure how to take that.

"And maybe because I want to bed you."

"You want to bed me?"

"Yes, I want to show you fifteen different reasons why being with an older man will rock your world in ways that will make you never look at a younger man again."

"Oh." My eyes widened and I took a deep gulp from the water glass on the table. This was like no date I'd ever been on before. This man was seducing me with his words. And his eyes were undressing me. I'd never been this turned on in my life. Never! And he hadn't even touched me. In that moment, he could have been twenty-five or fifty-five. It didn't matter to me. This was the most arousing situation I'd ever been in.

"Is that all you have to say?"

He was so cocky that I immediately decided that he was a man that needed to be taught a lesson.

"Well, I was a little bit surprised that you only had fifteen different reasons why being with an older man would rock my world. I've a feeling a thirty-year-old man could give me at least twenty."

"Well, then I guess you should go and find a thirty-year-old man to have a date with." He picked up his tumbler nonchalantly and took another sip as if he wouldn't be bothered at all if I left the table.

"Well, then, maybe I should." Feeling more disappointed than I should have, I decided to be a little crazy. Well, let's be honest, I'm already a bit crazy. A little bit more crazy. "Unless you really want to show me why I'm wrong."

"Unless I really want to show you why you're wrong?"

"Well, obviously, Charlotte and Max thought the two of us that would connect. Unless of course, Charlotte just wanted to set me up with anyone because I haven't gotten laid in what feels like years." I paused as I talked without thinking about my words actually meant. I couldn't quite believe I was flirting with this man. "Not that I need to get laid, of course. I'm an independent woman and all that."

"And independent woman can take care of themselves, right?"

"Exactly!" I exclaimed and then narrowed my eyes at him. "What does that mean?"

"What does what mean?" He looked at me with a confused expression but I could see the twinkle in his eyes. Was he making fun of me?

"You know," I said feeling annoyed.

"And so do you ..." He paused. "What was your name again?"

"You forgot?"

"Does that make you upset?"

"No, I couldn't care less," I lied. I was pretty miffed that he hadn't remembered. Was I not memorable? Or did he just not think I was hot? I mean I wasn't a supermodel, but I was attractive. Men looked at me when I made an effort and dressed nicely and wore makeup.

"Sure."

"What does that mean?" I narrowed my eyes at him and he looked amused.

"This is the reason why I don't date younger women." He gave me a look. "You have no idea what you want, and you play so many games that you have no idea if you're coming or going."

"I don't play games." I glared at him indignantly.

"Sure you don't, Little Miss Muffet." He looked at his watch. "As great as it has been—"

"I can show you I don't play games." I leaned over and pulled an ice cube out of his glass and then put it between my lips and sucked on it as I imagined some vamp would do in a porno movie. My lips were freezing and going numb, but I didn't blanch, even though I had to admit I felt like a bit of a fool. I let the water from the ice drip onto my hand and then I took the ice cube out and licked the droplets off of my skin, my eyes never leaving his face. His eyes narrowed as I sat back up and then swallowed the rest of the ice cube, trying carefully not to chew it as my sensitive teeth were going crazy. The brain freeze that followed was worth it, though, when he smiled.

"Maybe I'm wrong, then. Maybe you don't play games. What do you say we get out of here?"

"Maybe." I gulped. Could I really do this?

My phone beeped at that moment and I looked down to see a text from my ex, Jack. I could feel my body growing warm as I saw his name on my screen. What the hell was he doing texting me? I hadn't heard from him in a year, when he'd dumped me on our one-year anniversary date dinner because he wasn't sure if he wanted to be in a committed relationship any longer. He'd actually asked if I would mind if we saw other people. I promptly burst into tears. He looked apologetic, but said he wanted to see other people, I'd thrown my rum and Coke into his face and gone home. We hadn't communicated since. A part of me had hoped that he would take a long walk off of a short pier and that I'd see him on the news.

"Am I making you nervous?" the man across from me asked with a knowing grin and I shook my head slowly.

*Fuck you, Jack,* I thought to myself as I dismissed his name from my mind. I wasn't going to look at his text now or read it. I didn't care what he had to say. Not at all.

"No, you're not making me nervous. Why would you think you were making me nervous? Do I look like the sort of girl that could be nervous?" *Stop babbling, Emily. You sound like an idiot.*

"Do you want me to be honest?" His eyes bored into mine. "I think that you're a young girl who knows absolutely nothing about life, you don't know what you want and you're sitting here trying to convince both of us that you're not as scared as fuck as you flirt with me." He paused for a second. "I don't think you have the guts to go through with anything tonight. I don't think you even know what a good fucking feels like."

My jaw dropped at his use of the word fucking, and I could feel the heat radiating from my cheeks.

Preorder About Last Night here.

## ACKNOWLEDGMENTS

Firstly, I would love to thank my beta readers Joyce Black, Bonnie Ehmann, Ruth Mercado, Lorinda Cartwright, Elise Manee, Heather Massaro, Kelly Gunn, Faith Hunter, Sarah Milun, Michelle Manfre, Dea Brechtel, Kim Green, Annette Dauzat, Teresa Strudwick , Cheryl Petit, Danielle Williams, Sarah Mathyssen, Alicia Huckleby, Roxanne, Kelly Gunn, and Veronica Raab for all their feedback and help when writing this book.

Secondly, I would like to thank my friend and fellow author Sandi Lynn for motivating me to keep writing this book when I felt like I would never finish it in time.

Thirdly, I would like to thank all of my readers that enjoy my books and email me or send me a message. I love hearing from you all and it really makes my day. Thank you for being so supportive and amazing.

# FREE BOOK

Free Book

Join my mailing list here to receive a free book.

OTHER BOOKS BY J. S. COOPER

Along Came Baby
One Night Stand
The Ex Games
The Boyfriend Plan
The Playboy
Carry My Heart
Dante
The Bachelor's Games
Playing with Fire
Filthy Little LiesThe Kissing Bet

# ABOUT J. S. COOPER

About J. S. Cooper

Hi, my name is Jaimie Suzi, and I live in the Bay Area in California with my eight-year-old dog, Oliver. I love reading and writing romance and I am obsessed with board games. I grew up in London, England, and moved to the States my last year of high school. I love kayaking, otters, cupcakes, and Ed Sheeran. If you'd like to get in touch please email me at jscooperauthor@gmail.com or you can add me on Instagram at @jscooperauthor.

Printed in Great Britain
by Amazon